JUST PLAIN BOB

WIVES
Who Stray
BECOMING A SHARED WIFE, VOL. 3

EROTICA COLLECTION

WARNING

This book contains sexually explicit scenes and adult language. It may be considered offensive to some readers. This book is for sale to adults ONLY.

* * * * * * * * * * * * * * * * * *

Please store your files wisely where they cannot be accessed by underage readers.

Please feel free to send me an email. Just know that these emails are filtered by my publisher. Good news is always welcome.

Just Plain Bob - **justplainbob@awesomeauthors.org**

About the Publisher

4Fun Publishing, a member of **BLVNP Incorporated**, 340 S. Lemon #6200, Walnut CA 91789, info@blvnp.com / legal@blvnp.com
NOTE: Due to the highly emotional reaction of some people to works of erotic fiction, any email sent to the above address that contains foul language or religious references is automatically deleted by our anti-spam software and will not be seen. All other communications are welcome.

DISCLAIMER

Please don't be stupid and kill yourself. This book is a work of FICTION. Do not try any new sexual practice that you find in this book. It is fiction and not to be confused with reality. Neither the author nor the publisher or its associates assume any responsibility for any loss, injury, death or legal consequences resulting from acting on the contents in this book. Every character in this book is over 18 years of age. The author's opinions are not to be construed as the opinions of the publisher. The material in this book is for entertainment purposes ONLY. Enjoy.

Becoming a Shared Wife, Vol. 3

Wives Who Stray

Hot Erotica Collection

By: Just Plain Bob

© **Just Plain Bob 2014**

ISBN: 978-1-68030-056-7

"Is that all you want? To get turned on?"

Married couples have sexual fantasies. Husbands often fantasize about their wives having sex with other men.

When these fantasies turn into reality, there's no stopping from turning plain wives into wild and misbehaving partners. The husbands are turned on by the idea.

However, until how far can they handle? Turn the pages and find out.

Table of Contents

Wife 1: Alex

Wife 2: Bev

Wife 3: Connie

Wife 4: Dixie

Wife 5: Kathy

Wife 6: Linda

Wife 7: Mandy

Wife 8: Nancy

Wife 9: Hetty

Wife 10: Julie Hanson

BOOK SAMPLES:

Hazardous Wives - Becoming a Shared Wife, Vol. 2

Wife Sharing and Other Adventures - Becoming a Shared Wife, Vol. 1

Also by this Author

From the Author

An Open Letter from Just Plain Bob

Alex

I had never, not even once, thought about my wife having sex with another man. Alex is a very attractive woman and she does attract a lot of attention, but the only feelings that the attention generated in me were feelings of pride in that she had chosen me above all the others she could have had. And then everything turned to shit.

One evening six weeks ago, I was hosting a poker game at our house. When it is my turn to host the game, Alex always goes out for drinks with her girl friends and leaves us "crude" guys to our cards. Usually the game goes to mid-night, but on that particular night, two of the six guys were consistent winners and the other four of us lost interest in playing.

George said, "Hey, you guys want to see some porn tapes?"

Everybody said why not and George went out to his car to get them. We were in the middle of the first tape when the front door opened and Alex walked in – a good two hours earlier than expected. She made her usual noticeable entrance in her tight jeans and high heels and it was obvious as she made her way into the room to join us that she'd had quite a bit to drink. Sitting down, she recounted her uneventful evening and how disappointing and boring it had been. One of the guys said that our evening had pretty much sucked too, what with losing at cards and then watching porn tapes that were so bad that they didn't turn anybody on.

Alex giggled, "Is that all you want is to get turned on?"

Then to my absolute amazement, Alex stood up and proceeded to unzip her jeans and, without a word, let them drop to the floor. Standing in the middle of the floor with her back to us, she slowly slid her bikini panties down her long legs and stepped out of them. She casually tossed them over her shoulder and Jimmy caught them and brought them to his nose. He inhaled deeply, "God, but does she ever smell nice," and then the boys started passing her panties around and sniffing them.

It was obvious that Alex was getting turned on by the comments the boys were making about her panties and it didn't take much encouragement on their part to get Alex to finish undressing. Filled with courage (mostly liquid), Alex remarked that she was sorry that the porn tapes hadn't turned anybody on, but that she would give us all the real life eroticism we could handle as long as no one made any attempt to touch her. Everyone agreed to her condition and she started to do a slow dance in front of us.

Not once during all this had she so much as looked in my direction to see how I might be taking things.

She danced over to where George was sitting and put a foot up on the arm of his chair. Her pussy was only inches from his nose and she inserted a finger in it and brought it out and held it under George's nose. George inhaled deeply and Alex giggled and reached down to pat the growing lump in his trousers, "I said you couldn't touch, I didn't say anything about me." She repeated her actions for everyone in the room, doing me last. She still hadn't looked me in the eyes and when I reached out to grab her and pull her down in my lap and ask her just what in the hell she was doing she slapped my hand away, "No touching, and that includes you."

She danced over to the dining room table and got a candle out of the centerpiece and then lying down on the floor in front of us she spread her legs wide and slid the candle into her wet hole. By now, all the guys had their cocks out and they were jacking themselves off. Alex started working the candle in and out of her pussy, trying to match the rhythmic strokes of the men and suddenly Jimmy jumped up and ran over to her and shot his cum all over her belly and then he went back to his seat. As the hot cum splashed on her belly, she moaned and started fucking herself faster with the candle as the other guys got up and unloaded on her tummy. Further aroused by these offerings, Alex took the candle out of her pussy and tossed it to Mark who made a big show out of licking it clean. Alex crawled over to Jimmy and took the beer bottle out of his hand, lifted it to her mouth and drained it, and then lay back on the floor and started to use it as a massive dildo. She spread her red and swollen pussy lips and inserted the neck of the bottle. She was able to take all of the neck before sliding it back out, then she repeated the process half a dozen times before realizing that she wasn't going to get any more of the bottle in her. She put the bottle down and left the room.

Alex was back in less than a minute and she had a large dildo with her. Getting down on all fours, she sensually licked and sucked on the rubber cock while looking from face to face, but still avoiding me. Alex took the rubber dick in and out of her mouth several times while she fingered her pussy. The level of excitement grew as she took the dildo out of her mouth. Reaching down, Alex spread her swollen cunt lips and slowly worked the dildo into her pussy. Then she treated herself to a slow and deliberate fuck. As she continued to moan and rock back and forth, the guys all got up and one by one gave up their offerings to Alex. As the cum splattered and splashed on her body, she gave a load moan and had a shattering climax.

Lying there naked, Alex looked over at me for the first time since her display started. She flashed me a seductive smile and asked me to get her a drink of water. It took me a minute or two to find a clean glass, fill it and head back to the living room. I stopped in the doorway, frozen in my tracks by the sight in front of me. George was lying on his back with his hard cock pointing straight up into the air as Jimmy and Mark were lowering a twisting, turning Alex down on him. Bill had his cock in Alex's mouth and with his hands on the back of her head holding her he was fucking her face. I couldn't tell if Alex was in the throes of passion or fighting to get free, but if she was trying to break away from them, all thought of it vanished when her pubic bone smacked down onto George's. Alex gave a low moan around the pole in her mouth and then she started riding George's cock. I didn't know what to do. Part of me said, "That's your wife. You need to get in there and break this shit up," and part of me was so turned on at what I was watching that I had my cock in my hand and I was jacking myself off. Bill gave a loud grunt and white froth came out of Alex's mouth and then Bill stepped away and

Sam took his place. The rest of the evening was a blur as one after another of my friends fucked my wife. After an hour or so of fucking Alex on the living room floor, the guys picked her up and took her to the bedroom. I passed out about one and they were still going strong.

It was daylight when I woke up on the living room couch and at first, I thought that what had happened was just an erotic dream, but as I walked into the bedroom I saw that it hadn't been. George and Sam were sleeping on the bed with Alex between them. She was snoring softly and had a cock in each hand. I went downstairs and put on a pot of coffee and when it was ready, I went upstairs to wake everyone up only to find that they were already awake. Alex was on her hands and knees sucking George's cock while Sam was fucking her from behind. I watched until Sam shot his load and they switched positions before I went back downstairs. It was almost an hour later before the three of them came down. Over coffee, Alex told me that she and the guys had decided that I would be the permanent host for the poker games from now on and that she wouldn't be going out with the girls anymore.

"It's just so much more interesting here."

I asked if I had any say in the matter and she said no, "You had your chance to say something last night and you didn't. By not breaking things up when you could have you let the Genie out of the bottle. Genie found out she likes being out of the bottle and she is not going back in."

I guess the poker games are still going on at my house. I wouldn't know since I don't live there anymore. I had to change jobs and find a new circle of friends because I couldn't stand to look at my old ones anymore. Alex calls me on the average of once a day begging me to talk to her, but as much as I love her and miss her until this afternoon, I just hung up on her. This afternoon, I told her not to waste any more time calling me until she puts the Genie back into the bottle. I don't think I'll hear from her again.

Bev

Bev and I had been married almost fifteen years before the desire to see her with another man hit me. It happened at a family wedding reception where the drinks were flowing freely. It was halfway through the evening, everyone had swallowed enough to be mellow and Bev was on the dance floor with some guy from the bride's side of the family. I could tell from the way that the man held Bev and the way he moved his hands over her body, that what he wanted was to get her out of the building and onto the back seat of his car.

Bev had just enough booze in her that she wasn't objecting to the man's roaming hands and I began to wonder if he could get her outside and what would Bev do if he did? Then of course I wondered what I would do if it happened and the more I wondered, the more I thought that I would do nothing except watch. Why would I do otherwise? Bev has had more passes made at her over the years than I could count and she has always turned them away. If all of a sudden, she let it go too far, wouldn't I do more harm than good by rushing in to say "stop that?" The man did maneuver her outside and they did swap tongues for several minutes, but as soon as he got his hand under her skirt, she slapped him and came back inside. I was surprised to find that I was disappointed that it didn't go further.

On the way home that night, I asked her if she'd ever thought about having sex with another man and she laughed and said:

"All the time baby, all the time. I've even come close a time or two. I almost did it tonight."

Her answer caught me totally off guard because quite frankly I had expected here to say no.

"What happened tonight?" I asked.

She described what had happened with the man she had been dancing with (not knowing that I had seen it all) and said:

"If he had been a little more patient and had taken his time he just might have been my first."

I was shaken by her matter of fact attitude and even more shaken up when she slid over next to me and said:

"Why baby? Does the idea of me with another man excite you?"

She put her hand on my cock, which just happened to be rock hard, and giggled:

"My oh my. Maybe I should have let Chuck score tonight then you could have had sloppy seconds. Does the thought of that turn you on? Would you really like to slide your cock into me after another man has fucked me?"

I looked over at her, "You really would have done it if he had gone slower?"

She gave my leg a pat and said:

"No baby. Someday when the kids are grown up and gone maybe I will, but until then you will have to settle for being my only lover."

After that, human nature being what it is, every time I saw Bev talking to a guy, I wondered what she would look like fucking him.

~~***~~

Seven more years went by and then finally, we were alone. For the last seven years, I had fantasized about Bev having sex with other men and surprisingly enough she was the one who brought it up. One week after our youngest was married, Bev said, "Remember that little talk we had on the way home from Sarah's wedding?"

When I nodded yes she said, "I'm ready to go for it now. Do you think you can handle it?"

I shrugged my shoulders and she said, "Hey sweetie, we need to be on the same page here. Some of the guys I want to sleep with are friends of yours and two of them are related to you. Before I do anything I've got to be sure that it won't hurt us."

That made me stop and think. I'd always assumed that if she tried on anybody it would be some one that we knew and that she liked, but two of my relatives? That I wasn't sure I could handle and I told Bev that.

"Who are the two relatives?"

"Your brother and your cousin Al."

"Why them?"

"I don't really know other than animal magnetism. Both of them have hit on me and I suppose that might have something to do with it."

"My brother and my cousin have hit on you?"

Bev laughed, "Honey, all of your male relatives have hit on me at one time or another including your father."

"So what you are telling me is that you don't expect any problem in getting laid. Who is going to be first and when is it going to happen?"

She grinned, "The first will be the next one to hit on me. Then, when will be the first available opportunity? Are you absolutely sure that you are okay with it?'

I said yes and told her to go for it.

~~***~~

It happened sooner than I expected. When I got home from work the next day Bev hollered at me from the bedroom and told me to come up stairs. I walked into the bedroom and found Bev naked on a messed up bed. She spread her legs and I could see her cum soaked pussy hairs:

"I did it baby, I was a slut today. Come and get your sloppy seconds."

As I undressed she told me what had happened. My cousin Al had returned the floor jack that he had borrowed and Bev had asked him if he wanted to stay for a cup of coffee. They had sat at the kitchen table and sipped coffee and then Al had made a halfhearted pass at Bev and she had surprised him by getting up and going over to him and sitting on his lap.

"What do you have in mind Al? You want to fuck me? You want to take me upstairs and fuck me on my bed? You want me to suck your cock? Come on Al, just say it. I won't do it unless you tell me what you want."

Al had finally managed to get his shit together, at least enough to tell Bev that yes indeed, he did want to take her to her bed and fuck her. She had taken him by the hand and had led him upstairs.

"He fucked me three times sweetie and he just left so it should be good and sloppy for you."

It was. It was wet and sloppy and hot and it felt great.

"Come on baby, fuck me, fuck me hard. Make me forget Al's hard cock baby, fuck me and make me forget Al."

And I did my best to do what she was asking. I don't believe that I have ever fucked Bev as hard as I did that night or as many times. I fell asleep around midnight, totally exhausted.

Bev was still asleep when I went to work the next morning and I spent most of the day at work wondering what was in store for me when I got home that night. I rushed home to find Bev in the kitchen fixing dinner. She saw the look on my face and said:

"Sorry baby, no slut here today. Do you really expect me to fuck someone every day from now on? Not going to happen baby, just not going to happen."

~~***~~

It was two weeks before it happened again. We were at a birthday party for my brother and about an hour into it Bev came up to me and said:

"If you don't see me for a while, don't worry about it. Birthday boy asked me what I was going to give him for a present. I asked him what he wanted and he told me so I am going to slip off and see that he gets it."

She kissed me, "Think about me letting a hard cock slide into my pussy. Think about the mouth that just kissed you sucking another man's cock and think how hot, wet and sloppy my cunt is going to be when we get home."

Well, she was wrong about that part, we never made it home, but we did almost make it to jail. When we got in the car to go home that night, Bev slid over next to me and said:

"Kiss me baby," and when I did she said, "Could you taste him? He came in my mouth twice. Could you tell? He came three times in other places too."

She started to describe what she and my brother had done together and I couldn't hold off any longer. I pulled over to the side of the road, pushed Bev back on the seat and started fucking her. She felt loose and sloppy, but I didn't care. My cock was soaking in her hot box and that's all that mattered. I was right on the edge of cumming when all of a sudden red, yellow and blue lights seemed to fill the car.

Before Bev and I could sit up, there was a tap on the window and a flashlight beam illuminated us. We ended up getting two tickets; one for indecent public behavior and one for disturbing the peace, which I thought was terribly ironic because that's what they did to us – disturbed the piece. When we pulled away from the side of the road, we were quiet for the first couple of miles and then Bev started to giggle and by the time we got home we were both laughing about it. When we got home, we raced for the bedroom and then fucked like rabbits until two in the morning.

~~***~~

The next day was a workday for me and Bev was still asleep when I left the house. That night when I got home, I found Bev in a short black cocktail dress and wearing high heels.

"Your dinner is on the stove sweetie. I've got a hot date tonight so don't wait up for me."

I asked her what was going on and she said, "I'm going to get fucked tonight baby. I'll tell you all about it in the morning. I'm running late and I have to go. Don't wait up."

She kissed me and she left. Telling me that she was going to get fucked and then telling me not to wait up only guaranteed that I would be up waiting for her no matter how late she came home. It was three in the morning when she walked in the door. Lipstick smeared, hair mussed, runs in her nylons and cum stains on her dress – she looked like she'd had a great time. She was surprised to see me awake and she grinned:

"Ready for sloppy seconds lover?"

I was and it was six in the morning before I couldn't get it up any more.

~~***~~

We were lying next to each other and staring up at the ceiling when Bev said:

"I lied to you baby. You didn't get sloppy seconds - it was sloppy thirds."

I got up on an elbow and looked at her and she said, "That's right baby, I had not one, but two cocks in me tonight. God I was such a slut. You should have seen me with a cock in my pussy and one in my mouth. At one time I even had one in my ass and one in my pussy; it was wild baby, it was wild and crazy and I want to do it again."

She had gotten a phone call from one of the cops who had written us the tickets the night before. He told her that if she was willing to go out with him he could find a way to make the tickets go away. She had agreed and he had taken her to dinner. After dinner they had gone into the bar where they "just happened" to run into his desk sergeant and the two of them told her that a couple of hours in a hotel room would make the tickets disappear and Bev had agreed to it.

"They couldn't get enough of me honey. If they hadn't needed to leave to go home to their wives, I'd still be on my back in that hotel room. I loved it honey, I really loved having two men working me over."

Listening to her story had gotten me hard again and I rolled over on top of her and started fucking her again. As I slipped my cock into her hot wet hole I told her that I was going to call in sick and we would just stay in bed and fuck.

"No honey, you can't stay home today."

"Why not?"

"Because I have one more thing to do to get rid of those tickets."

"What do you mean?"

"I only took care of one of the cops who were in the patrol car that night. The other one couldn't get away from his wife last night - he's going to come here today."

"It's settled then. I'm staying home and I'll be in the closet."

"I don't know sweetie. It's one thing for me to fuck other guys and then tell you about it, but I don't know if I can do it with you watching."

"We'll find out today then, won't we?"

The cop, when he arrived, would be the one getting sloppy seconds because I just could not keep my hands off Bev that morning. When we finished screwing, she went and took a shower and when she came back into the room, I pulled her down and fucked her again. She took another shower and managed to get her makeup, high heels and nylons on before I pulled her down again. By ten o'clock, I had fucked her four times and was in the middle of fucking her for a fifth when the doorbell rang. Bev pushed me away:

"Sorry honey, you'll just have to save it for later."

I was in the closet when Bev came back into the room with a guy who couldn't have been as old as our youngest son. If it weren't for the uniform he was wearing, along with the gun and the other stuff hanging off him, I would have bet he was still in high school. He seemed to be a little on the nervous side, probably new to the force and not used to fucking housewives who want to get out from under tickets. Bev sensed it and took the initiative. She reached for the buckle on his equipment belt:

"Come on lover, let's get rid of this stuff. It's your other gun that I'm interested in."

She helped him undress and then she took his cock in her hand and led him over to the bed. She pushed him down so that he was sitting on the edge of the bed and then she knelt down between his legs:

"Let's start with a nice slow and easy blowjob."

She took him in her mouth and started to suck him off. After a couple of minutes, she stood up and pushed him on his back and then she mounted him and I watched from the closet as she worked herself up and down on his stiff pole. My cock was rock hard and I wanted to leave the closet and put my cock in her mouth or her ass, but I didn't – I just watched and suffered as she fucked him and sucked him for the next two hours.

Just about the time that I was hoping the kid would leave, the doorbell rang. Bev was sucking the kid's cock and she ignored the interruption, but whoever was at the door was insistent and finally she got up, put on a robe and went down to see who it was. Three or four minutes later, she came back into the room with two guys and she looked over at the closet with a "sorry honey" kind of look. I recognized one of the two as the cop who wrote us the two tickets and I guessed that the other one was the desk sergeant.

The next three hours was orgy time. Bev was used in every conceivable position and in every available hole and combination of holes. I blew my load against the closet door three times and more than anything, I wanted to get out of the closet and videotape what was going on. Finally the three men had to leave and they started to get dressed as Bev lay on the bed and watched. The sergeant hung back until the other two were gone and then he said:

"If you want I can quietly put out your name, tag number and description at roll call and see to it you never get stopped for a ticket ever again. All it will cost you is seeing me a couple of times a week."

Bev glanced over at the closet and then said, "Sounds like an offer a girl would be silly to refuse, but it has to include my husband."

"Done!"

"Friday good for you? Same time?"

The front hadn't quite closed and I was out of the closet and heading for the bed, but Bev pushed me away, "Not now baby, please, not now. I'm so sore that I don't even know if I'll be able to walk to the bathroom. Let me soak in the tub for a while, okay?"

Not what I really wanted to hear, especially after what I had just watched and with a rock hard cock in my hand, but I had to back off. I helped her off the bed and into the bathroom and ran her a tub full of hot water. Then while she soaked, I took care of my hard on the old fashioned way – by hand – and then I went and cleaned up the mess I'd made in our closet.

~~***~~

Bev became quite the slut after that. True to what she had said, anyone who made a pass at her that she thought she might like got fucked. If we went to a party she would likely end up on someone's backseat. We went out dancing one night and I got up to go to the bathroom and when I came back all I found was a cocktail napkin that said, "See you later." It was two o'clock the next afternoon before she came home.

I've watched from the closet as a steady stream of friends, neighbors and relatives paraded through my bedroom. Bev has fucked my brother, all three of my cousins, both of my uncles and she swears that she will nail my father before Christmas. She told me that she planned on fucking every male member of my family before she gets too old to fuck and maybe a few of her own. I laughed and said, "Not every male I hope. You will leave our sons alone, right?"

I said it as a joke, but Bev got a weird look on her face and I hope I read it wrong. She wouldn't, would she?

Connie

All I was doing was giving my wife a gift. Giving her something that she would truly enjoy and remember for the rest of her life. But what I did was cause her to become a slut and in the process I most probably destroyed our twenty-five year marriage.

Connie and I married right out of college and she has kept me the happiest man in the world for almost twenty-five years. She has been loving, caring, supportive, a fantastic lover and my best friend and I wanted to do something for her to show her just how much I loved and appreciated her. The gift I gave her was no ordinary gift. I loved her enough to swallow my pride, bury my ego and give her something that I knew she had always wanted and something that I personally could not deliver. I gave her another man. More specifically, I gave her a man with a large cock.

Connie and I had a marvelous sex life. Granted, it did slacken after the first full bloom of marriage, going from nightly (sometimes two or three times) to six nights, then five and eventually to four, but we still made love at least four times a week and usually more than once. Other times, we might go all week without making love once and then go seven or eight times over the weekend. Whatever, we still wanted each other and never got in a rut.

One of the things that kept our sex life interesting was pornography. Early in our marriage, we went to a party one night and downstairs in the recreation room they had a porn video playing on the TV. Neither Connie nor I had ever seen anything like that before and it turned us in. When we got home, we spent the rest of that night and most of the next day doing what we saw on that tape. We tried every position that we could and tried to duplicate everything we had seen. That night was the first time for either of us trying anal sex and Connie found that she enjoyed it and it became a regular part of our lovemaking. From that night on, we would rent a porno tape at least once a week and then try out every move and position we saw. I know that to most people the tapes all look the same, but Connie and I always seemed to find something new in each of them.

The one thing those tapes all had in common was that the actors all had such large cocks. In fact, it is probably a given that if you are a man and you want to work in the porno industry, you have to have a bigger than average dick. Playing sports in high school and serving in the Army meant a lot of time spent in shower rooms with other guys and so I know that I'm pretty average as far as cock size goes. I saw some larger, and quite a few smaller, but most guys seemed to have about what I had – six or so inches. Even though I have always satisfied Connie, hardly ever failing to bring her to orgasm, she was still aware of the fact that there were bigger cocks out there in the world.

We would be watching a movie and all of a sudden she would say something like, "My God, look at the size of that thing. How in God's name can she take all that?" Once when I asked her what she wanted for Christmas she laughed and said, "Peter North would be nice." I got her a Jeff Stryker dildo instead. Some time later, I found an ad in a man's magazine for poster sized porno stars and I ordered all sixteen of the male posters and gave Connie one on every Christmas and birthday until I ran out. She always got a kick out of them and said:

"You know that someday you are going to have to get me the real thing."

Also over the years, I gave her a collection of super-sized dildos and she always accepted them with good humor, but even though it was always treated as a joke I knew that Connie secretly wondered what a big one would really be like. After twenty-five years, I decided to give her the experience. I brought the subject up about a month before our anniversary. I told her what I wanted to do for her and she threw her arms around me and thanked me for loving her so much that I would be willing to do something like that for her:

"But as curious as I am I can't do it."

So I asked her why not.

"Because I can't do it with someone I know and I won't do it with someone I don't. Thanks lover, but I'll stick with you. You haven't let me down yet."

I should have dropped it right there and I probably would have if I hadn't rented a video a couple of days later. Watching it, I saw how excited she got when the huge cocked star started using his tool on his co-star and I made the decision to see that she had the experience. One of the things that we occasionally did was engage in mild bondage. Sometimes I would be the submissive one and other times she would take that part. I decided to use one of those times to give her my gift.

I belong to a health club and I knew several guys that were also members who could fill the bill. One had the advantage of being a good friend and so I decided to ask him. It took some courage on my part to approach him and broach the subject. He was amused, but not surprised, as I was not the first husband who had approached him seeking stud services. He agreed and we worked out the details.

That evening, I would sneak him into the house while Connie was in the kitchen fixing dinner and he would wait in our bedroom until he heard us coming and then he would get into the closet. I would blindfold Connie, pull her arms behind her back and cuff her with some fur-lined handcuffs. I would get on her knees with her head on a pillow and start making love to her. When she started moaning he would come out of the closet, put a little KY on his cock and I would step back and he would take my place. He wouldn't speak and I wouldn't let Connie take off her blindfold. Other than that we would play it by ear.

It went off like clockwork. I had Connie in position, ass up on the edge of the bed and I was fucking her slowly from behind. We had started out using a few of her toys and they were lying on the bed next to her.

After several minutes of slowly stroking into her I began to pick up the pace and Connie began to moan, "Oh baby, oh baby, fuck me, oh god yes" and I saw Stan come out of the closet and move up behind me. His cock, all eleven inches of it, glistened with the lube he had on it and I nodded at him to get ready. I stepped back from Connie and she cried out, "Don't stop baby, I need it."

Stan moved behind her, lined himself up with Connie's slit and slowly pushed himself into her.

"Oh baby, which one are you using?"

Connie thought that I had pulled out to grab one of her big dildos.

"Oh god baby, yes, yes, yes, oh so good," as Stan surged into her and then Stan placed his hands on her hips and started to fuck her hard. Connie suddenly realized that it was no toy.

"Oh god baby, what are you doing to me? What's going on baby, oh god, oh god, oh Jesus, so good, so good, don't stop, please… god, don't stop… fuck me, fuck me hard, fuck meeeeeee!!!" she screamed as she had an orgasm.

Stan had a steady tempo going, neither too fast or too slow, and Connie had orgasm after orgasm and her moans were on long stream of words with no discernable gaps between them. The room was filled with her moans and cries, "fuck me… fuck me… fuck me… oh… Jesus, don't stop… don't stop… don't stop!"

Stan started fucking her harder and then Connie screamed and had the largest orgasm I had ever seen and Stan erupted and his strokes slowed and finally stopped. Connie's cries subsided and she laid there, head buried in the pillow moaning.

"Oh god, oh god, oh god."

Stan looked over at me with a "what now?" expression. I honestly hadn't thought any farther than we had just gone, but it was obvious to me that Connie had enjoyed it immensely and so I made the decision to press on. I pointed at Connie lying there and indicated that Stan should stick his cock in Connie's mouth. He nodded and moved up to her head, knelt next to her and poked his cock at her lips. Connie opened her mouth and her tongue came out and licked the cock head, sliding around it as if to ascertain its size and then she gave a low moan and her lips closed around it.

Stan fucked her three times that night before slipping away and I didn't take the cuffs and blindfold off Connie until I heard Stan's car pull out of the drive. Connie looked up at me.

"Good God baby, who was it?"

I smiled and said, "All you need to know is that he was my gift to you."

I got in bed with her and we fell asleep in each other's arms.

Of course, that wasn't the end of it. Over the course of the next several days, Connie attempted to find out who her mystery lover was and I wouldn't tell her. Finally I said, "Why do you want to know, so you can call him and ask him to come back?"

She looked down and said yes. I looked at her for several seconds and then I told her that I would see what I could do. That afternoon, I called Stan and asked him how he felt about a return engagement and he was all for it. He had been immensely turned on by the fact that he had fucked Connie and she hadn't known who he was. I asked him if he was free the following night and he said yes.

That night, I stopped at the same adult book store where I rented the tapes and found just what I was looking for – a leather hood with a drawstring closure at the neck and an opening in the mouth area. When I got home I handed it to Connie.

"He will be here tomorrow night, but you will have to wear this. He doesn't want you to know who he is (actually I didn't want her to know) because you know him and he wants to avoid awkwardness when you are together in social situations."

That night, Connie and I had some of our most intense sex in years. Connie even talked me into staying home from work the next day and she wouldn't leave me alone, but at three in the afternoon she pushed me away.

"No more. I want you to have something left for after he leaves."

At seven o'clock, Stan entered the bedroom to find Connie spread out and waiting for him. She was wearing the hood, but there were no handcuffs that night as I wanted Connie to be able to let herself go and get the utmost enjoyment out of the evening. It was a long one. Stan fucked Connie four times and she sucked him back to life twice. While he was dressing to leave Connie said, "Next time baby, can I let him have my ass?"

Next time? Had I given her the gift that keeps on giving? For the first time I was beginning to think that I might just have fucked up. I looked at Stan and he mouthed the words that he was okay with it. I took a minute to consider the possibilities and then said, "You suffer a lot of discomfort when I take your ass. I know it goes away when we really get into it, but his will cause you more than just discomfort - his will cause you real pain. He will hurt - a lot!"

"I know baby, but I just have to try it."

I looked over at Stan and saw he was waiting for an answer.

"Friday good for you?"

He nodded and I said, "Okay, Friday it is."

When Stan was gone, I took the hood off Connie and she pulled me down and kissed me. Then she looked at me with a face full of wonder:

"I honestly don't believe that there is another man in the world who loves his wife enough to do for her what you are doing for me," and she pulled me down and we made love.

I think Friday was the beginning of Connie's slide into slutdom. Before she put the hood on she told me that she wanted to try some other things that we had never done.

"Tonight I want to try a threesome. I want you to join in, please? Please do it for me?"

I did and I have to say that I did enjoy it almost as much as Connie did. Stan was there from seven to two-thirty and Connie had us doing everything two guys to do to a girl. She even sat on my cock and bent forward while Stan fucked her ass. I can't say that I was turned on feeling his cock rub against mine through the thin membrane, but it drove Connie wild. After Stan was gone, Connie and I made love twice more and then we fell asleep. Connie woke me with a blowjob in the morning and then spent the better part of Saturday and Sunday trying to fuck me to death.

Sunday night, Connie asked, "Can we do it again? Please baby, please?"

For the next two months, Stan and I did our best to try and satisfy Connie on the average of twice a week. Following every one of those nights Connie couldn't leave me alone, not that I was complaining. I gradually noticed that it wasn't only after nights with Stan that she couldn't leave me alone – it was now almost all the time. I asked her one night what was the reason for her increased sexual appetite and she said that she didn't know, but it seemed like the more sex she got, the more she wanted.

"Why? Are you getting tired of me?"

I assured her that I wasn't, but that I was a little worried that I might not be able to keep up with her. She giggled and said:

"If you get to that point we can always have my mystery man visit more often."

I began to wonder if that is what is what it was all about – getting me to get Stan more involved.

It was two weeks later when I found out how badly my gift to Connie had backfired on me. It was a Sunday and I was sitting in one of the stalls in the locker room of the health club when someone came in and said:

"Are we on for tomorrow?"

I recognized the voice; it was Ron, a friend of mine. Then the voice of another friend said:

"Yeah, I've already made arrangements to take the afternoon off. I just wish we could find some way to get Connie out of the house at night. I'd like to be able to spend more than just a couple of hours with her."

There was some more conversation before they left, mostly about what they had done to Connie and were planning on doing to her the next day. Was it my Connie that they were talking about? No! It couldn't be. It had to be one of the other Connie's that we know.

But I was parked down the street from my house the next day. By two in the afternoon, I had convinced myself that I was right; it was one of the other Connie's that we knew. At 2:11:36, I turned the ignition key and started up the car to leave. At 2:11:51, I shut off the engine as Ron's Tahoe pulled into our drive. Two minutes, later a Honda Accord pulled in behind him and both men went into the house and I settled in to wait. I knew that they would have to be out by four forty-five at the latest to give Connie time to get ready for me to come home.

I was close – they came out of the house at four-fifty and I pulled into the drive two minutes after they were gone. I went straight up the stairs and directly to the bedroom. Connie's back was to me and she was wearing thigh high nylons that looked like they had been through a war and I could see a trace of cum on her inner thigh. She was taking the sheets off the bed.

"Going to hide the evidence from me?" I asked.

She turned, surprise on her face, and then just froze like a deer caught in headlights. Standing the way, she was I could see her matted pubic hair, soaked with cum and it somehow excited me. I considered pushing her down on the bed and fucking her, but I didn't. I was pissed; I was upset, but not for any of the reasons that people might expect. I wasn't upset because she was fucking other guys – I was upset because she hadn't shared it with me. I turned my back on her and went downstairs.

It was half an hour before she came downstairs and into the family room where I sat channel surfing. She had put on a robe, but was still wearing her cum stained nylons. She sat down on the other end of the couch.

"Are you mad?"

I turned and looked at her, amazed at the question, "Am I mad? Good God woman, of course I'm mad!"

Despite looking contrite she fired back, "Well, it's your own god damned fault."

I was incredulous, "My fault? How in the hell is your fucking two of my friends my fault?"

"You wouldn't tell me who my mystery man was and so I had to try and find him on my own. I knew from what you said that I knew him. If you had just told me who he was I wouldn't have had to fuck eleven different guys in the last six weeks to try and find him."

I looked at her, stunned, as what she had said registered on me. "Eleven? Eleven of our friends?"

"Yeah, and I still haven't found him" and then she chuckled, "Of course I don't care if I find him now or not."

I just sat there shaking my head; eleven of my friends going behind my back and fucking my wife.

"What did you do? Line them all up and ask them to show you their cocks so you could measure them? Or did you just invite them all over for a gangbang?"

"No silly, I did them one at a time."

Then how did you end up with two guys here today if you only do them one at a time?"

"You know? I thought you just happened to come home early."

I told her about what I'd overheard and how I'd been parked just down the block to see if it was true.

"I had two in here today because with the exception of you baby, all men are assholes. The guys I screwed blabbed about it and they started to show up in bunches. Today it was two, last Friday it was three and last Tuesday I actually had five here."

It was too much for me. I got up, grabbed my coat and headed for the door.

"Where are you going?"

"Out!"

"Why are you acting like this? You're the one who brought another man home to fuck me. Him or the others, what's the difference?"

I turned and looked at her, "The difference Connie, is that we shared the experience when I brought Stan home with me. Stan was a gift I gave you out of love and we shared it. What you did was go behind my back and fuck around on me and if you can't tell the difference between the two then I feel sorry for you."

I'm spending the night in a motel. I don't have a clue what tomorrow is going to bring, but there is a better than even chance that I'm not going to like it.

Dixie

The worst night of my life was the night I gave myself to a man other than my husband. The best night of my life was when I confessed and my husband forgave me.

I've always been somewhat of a prude. When I was a teen, I never kissed a boy until the fifth date, I never allowed a boy to touch my breasts and if a boy put a hand on my leg he got slapped. I had several boyfriends in college, but I made sure that every one of them knew that I was saving myself for marriage. I didn't smoke, I didn't drink and the fastest way to insure that I would never see you again was to swear in my presence.

I went to my marriage bed a virgin and then I underwent a transformation. I was still a prude everywhere else, but I became an absolute sex maniac in my own bedroom. I married a man with some sexual experience (a lot of it apparently) and as he began to teach me everything he knew I became his absolute slut. If Bert wanted me to do something, I did it, no questions asked. In the space of three weeks, I went from virgin to a woman who would take my husband's cock anywhere he wanted to put it. I loved sucking his cock, I loved it when he fucked me in my ass, went wild when he was in my pussy and I went absolutely nuts when he ate my pussy. When he got home from work more often than not, I was naked and waiting for him and that was something that never wore off. Six years into our marriage, I still couldn't keep my hands off of him.

I took a lot of ribbing from my girlfriends over the fact that I had waited so much longer than they did to 'give it up' but I still think it was worth it. After six years of marriage, I'm getting screwed almost every night and most of them are complaining about only getting laid twice and sometimes three times a week. I can't prove that my saving myself for marriage is responsible for my continued great sex life, but I believe it.

Most of my friends lost their virginity by the time they were sixteen while I waited until I was twenty-two. I think they were jaded by the time they got married and it showed in their attitudes and approach to sex. Bert says nothing turns a guy off more than thinking a girl is just going through the motions to get it over with. I think my friends are looking at it as a chore. You know about chores, right? You don't want to do them and so you put them off until you finally have to do them and that's what I think was happening between my friends and their husbands.

~~***~~

My company Christmas party was held on a Tuesday night during the second week of December. Bert couldn't go with me because of his work schedule and not going was not an option for me. Parties at my company were more political events than social ones and to not attend was detrimental to your career. Besides, the annual bonuses were handed out at that party and I need to know how much mine was so I would know what I had to work with when I went shopping for Bert's Christmas present.

The luck of the draw put me at a table with two couples and Brad and Charlie. Brad and Charlie were both single and Charlie was my section leader. When I sat down, Charlie asked me what I was drinking and I told him anything that was non-alcoholic and he got up to get me a drink. When he came back he handed me a glass of orange juice.

"I had them put a little juice from the bottle of maraschino cherries in it so it would have a slightly tart taste."

I sipped it and it wasn't bad. We had dinner and Brad and Charlie kept my glass full of juice and they kept putting weird things in it to keep it from tasting like plain old OJ. What I didn't learn until later, much later, was that what they were doing was doctoring the juice to hide the taste of the vodka they were lacing the drink with.

When dinner was over, we sat through the speeches given by the CEO, the VP of this and the regional manager of that and anyone else who was deemed important enough to have something to say and then the bonus checks were handed out. I looked at mine and was surprised to see that it was almost three times more than I had thought it would be. Charlie saw the look on my face.

"I gave you a pretty good evaluation. You deserved it, but even though you earned it on your own I still think you should thank me by giving me this dance."

The band had started playing and I do love to dance and so I went out onto the floor with him. When I got back, Brad had me a fresh drink and then I had to dance with him and then Charlie wanted to dance again. I began to feel a little light-headed; I was hot and felt flushed, but I was having a good time and I thought that it might be the temperature of the room combined with some of the fast dances that were the cause.

More OJ and more dances and then I wasn't clear headed anymore. I heard snatches of conversations that I didn't understand, at least not until later. "...ready yet?" "...just a little mo..." "...room here?" "Got it this morni..." Then I was in an elevator and being held up by two men. Brad and Charlie I thought, but I wasn't really sure. I was picked up and carried down a long hallway and then I was lying on a bed and staring up at an unfamiliar ceiling. My head was swimming and voices were drifting in and out, "She is nice and..." "...long time for this" "Call it." "Heads" "You lucky bas..." I felt my legs being pulled apart, but I didn't know what was happening until I felt the hardness pushing into me.

~~***~~

How had I gotten home? I didn't remember Bert undressing me, but he must have. How else could he put himself in me? A voice, not Bert's, but a man's voice, "God is she tight." The hardness moved into me, a mouth fastened itself to mine and another mouth closed on my breast and fingers teased the nipple on my other breast. The hardness was insistent now, pushing and seeking to find something and I heard loud moaning sounds and then I realized that they were coming from me.

My body was responding to the attention it was getting from Bert's hands and mouth and I slowly realized that the hardness was Bert's cock and that he was making love to me. A voice floated into my head.

"Jesus, we just have to get some of this when she is sober."

"We will find a way."

I was out of it, but my body knew what was happening to it and my legs hooked behind Bert and my ass hunched up at him. Something was pushing at my mouth and then hands captured my twisting and turning head and held it still while Bert pushed his cock into my mouth. How could this be? How could Bert be in my pussy and my mouth at the same time? Oh God, what was happening to me?

Voices again, "...room service for coffee." "...sobered up." Then my pussy was flooded with warmth and the hardness in me left me and then the cock in my mouth left me and suddenly I felt hardness pushing into me again. Things were a little clearer now and I knew that the cock in my mouth had just invaded my pussy. How could Bert do all this?

Moments later, another cock pushed at my mouth and it was wet and sticky and I knew the taste. It must have been the one that was just in my pussy. The cock in my pussy was driving hard and I was responding with kicking legs and loud moans. Some of the fog lifted from my eyes and I saw Charlie looking down at me. Why was Bert letting Charlie fuck me? Was this all just a dream – a nightmare? Charlie was breathing hard, "Here it comes sweetie, here it comes," and again I felt a flood of warmth in the lower part of my body.

The cock in my mouth left me and then I felt another one enter me. The one that had just left my mouth? I lifted my head and looked around for Bert, but he wasn't there. I was nude – how did that happen? Why was Charlie naked and standing there looking at Brad fucking me? How did Brad get on me?

There was a knock at the door and Brad opened the door to find the room service waiter standing there with a cart. The waiter's eyes met mine and I saw the hunger in them. He pushed his cart into the room and as Charlie signed the bill, he saw the way the waiter was looking at me and he said:

"If you have the time, she's your tip."

The waiter started to strip as I leaned on my elbows and watched. The fog was lifting and I saw what was happening; how it happened escaped me, but I knew that I had just been fucked by two men and they had just given me to a third.

The waiter was naked now and walking toward me and I could not take my eyes off of his black cock. By now, I was fully aware that Brad and Charley had fucked me, but I hadn't seen them do it. But I saw the waiter's cock; I saw it coming toward me and I laid back and spread my legs and waited for it. I didn't protest, I didn't scream or fight, I just waited there for the waiter to put it in me.

As he entered me, I heard myself say, "That's it, put it in me, that's it, fuck me now, please fuck me."

When the waiter was gone, Charley and Brad did me again and then they poured black coffee into me until I was fully aware of my surroundings; my nakedness, their nakedness and the two erect cocks just waiting to be used again. They confessed to me what they had done and Charley said:

"But we are not apologizing. We have both wanted you since the day you got hired on and tonight we took a shot and got lucky."

Brad grinned and said, "And it was worth the wait," as he pushed me back on the bed and moved between my legs.

"Wait!" I said as I reached for the bedside phone. I called home and when Bert answered I said:

"I'm sorry honey, but I tried a few mixed drinks tonight and I don't think I'm in any shape to drive home. I got a room at the hotel. I think I'm all right baby, but I don't want to take a..." at that point in the conversation, Brad drove home and I moaned. "Nothing honey, just my head hurts a little."

Brad was picking up speed and I managed to tell Bert that I loved him and hang up before he had a chance to hear me cry out, "Oh yes, oh god yes, fuck me, please fuck me."

Over the next three hours, Brad and Charlie made me into their slut. They did everything to me that two men could do to a woman and I rolled around on that bed and loved it. At one point, I was begging them, actually begging them to fuck me harder and Charley said:

"Maybe we should get the room service waiter back up here. Would you like that? Could you use a little more cock?"

I was on my hands and knees and Brad was fucking me from behind and I heard myself say:

"I don't care, just keep fucking me. Please don't stop fucking me."

Charlie called down to room service and ordered breakfast.

"Try to hang on baby. Help will be here soon," and he fed his cock into my mouth. I didn't hear the knock on the door and I didn't know that the waiter was in the room until his fat black cock was stuffed down my throat. Fifteen minutes later, I had all three of them in me at once and I was screaming out in pleasure.

At four in the morning, the boys were all fucked out and I couldn't get them up anymore. They dressed to leave and on the way out the door, Charlie looked at me.

"Can we do this again sometime?"

I just smiled at him and my head hit the pillow and I crashed.

I woke up in the morning extremely horny and as I remembered the previous evening, I got even hotter. The more I thought about what Brad and Charlie had done to me the hotter I got. I had planned on taking a shower and hurrying home to Bert, but the hotter I felt the less I wanted to wait to feed the hunger. The thought bounced around in my head for all of a minute and then I picked up the phone and called room service.

It was a different waiter this time and when I answered the door in all my naked Glory, his eyes almost popped out of his head. He pushed the cart into the room and I pushed the door shut behind him and then grabbed him and pulled him to the bed. I fucked him twice and sucked him once before I signed the bill with Charlie's name and let him go.

~~***~~

As I showered, the guilt over cheating on Bert started to creep in. I knew that I had no control over how it started, but as the evening progressed and I became more and more aware, I made no move to stop anything. I had been a slut and I had spent a good part of the evening begging men to fuck me.

I did nothing to stop the first room service waiter and I certainly couldn't say that I didn't have control over what I had just done to the second. No, last night I had been a cock hungry slut, pure and simple. Could I hide my transgressions from Bert? Would he see the guilt written all over my face when I got home? Then I remembered something – I wasn't going home, at least not yet. This was a Wednesday and it was a workday for me. I glanced at the bedside clock and saw that if I hurried, I would only be half an hour late.

When I got to work, I felt as if every eye on the place was on me as I walked to my office. Did they know? Was it possible to look at a person and tell that she had gone from faithful wife to cock crazy slut? I just knew that everyone knew what I had done the previous night. The day went by slowly and I spent more and more time wondering how I would be able to face Bert when I got home.

About four in the afternoon, Charlie called me into his office and when I was inside, he got up and locked the door behind me.

"How are you feeling?" he asked.

I shrugged my shoulders. I mean how could I answer that? I had betrayed my husband, made a mockery of my wedding vows and what was worse – I ended up liking it.

Charlie said, "You really didn't do anything that you didn't want to do. I've seen it in you ever since you were hired in here. You had all that suppressed sexuality in you just waiting for a chance to break out. Brad and I just helped it break free."

He unzipped himself and took out his cock, "Look at it Dixie, look at it and tell me that last night was a terrible mistake and that it can never happen again. You can't, can you? You want to touch it, you want to taste it, and you want it in you again and again and again. If I'm wrong, just turn around and go."

I looked at his face and then down at his cock and slowly I went to my knees and reached for it. I sucked him until he made me get up on his desk and then he fucked me while I bit down on a rubber eraser to keep from crying out in pleasure. When he was done, he picked up the phone and pushed a button.

"She's on her way."

He hung up and said, "Brad is waiting for you in his office."

~~***~~

Driving home that night, I was in an absolute turmoil. I just knew that when I walked into the house that Bert would take one look at me and yell:

"You slut! You unfaithful slut."

What could I say to him? Could I say that it wasn't my fault? That I had gotten drunk and had been taken advantage of? Would he believe me? Would it even matter, or would it be a case of once a slut always a slut? And how could I possibly explain that I had agreed to meet Brad and Charlie at a motel the next day during lunch?

All my worrying was for naught. When I got home, Bert took me in his arms and kissed me. He told me that he missed me last night and had trouble sleeping alone. I fixed us some dinner and then when we were through eating, I told him my head still hurt from my first attempt at drinking and that I needed to go and soak in the tub for a while.

Bert didn't seem suspicious and I didn't seem to be giving off the scent of a slut, but I had cheated on him and I was going to do it again the next day and probably a lot more times after that. I did feel the guilt and I was surprised that I wasn't wearing it for Bert to see. In the tub, I tried to get as much of Brad and Charlie out of me as I could to keep Bert from finding anything that might make him wonder.

That night, Bert and I made love several times and when he finally fell asleep, I laid there looking up at the ceiling and wondered how I could love Bert as much as I did and still do what I had done and was going to do again.

~~***~~

Over the next six months, I was pretty much Brad and Charlie's sex toy. They took me on their desks at work, we met in motels during lunch, we stopped for drinks after work and they had me on their back seats. Once when Bert went out of town for three days, they spent two nights sleeping with me at my house and on one of those nights Charlie was fucking me and Brad was sucking on one of my breasts when Bert called. Charlie came in me and got out of the way so Brad could fuck me while Bert and I talked.

And Brad and Charlie weren't the only ones who got to fuck me during that time. They seemed to get a kick out of giving me to room service waiters, parking lot attendants and once they took me to a hotel room and I found five of our best customers waiting.

I don't know much longer it would have gone on had I not been finally hit with a severe case of guilt. I had always felt guilty about cheating on Bert, but I rationalized it away; I was giving him more than he could handle and he didn't know what I was doing so it hurt no one so I was able to hold the guilt at bay.

And then one afternoon during which Brad, Charley and I had taken the afternoon off from work and spent it in a hotel room, the guilt came crashing down on me and driving home I just could not stop crying. I was crying when I went into the house and when Bert asked me what was wrong I ran crying up to the bedroom and slammed the door behind me.

Bert came into the room and kept after me to tell him what was wrong and finally I did. I told him the whole sorry, sordid story about what had happened to me at the Christmas party, what I had become and what I had done since then. He listened in silence and then he got up and left the room. I threw myself down on the bed and cried myself into an exhausted sleep.

I woke up the next morning with Bert snuggled next to me and his arm around me. I was surprised because I was sure he would have slept in the spare bedroom or on the couch in the living room. As soon as I stirred he woke up and pulled me to him, buried his face in my neck and kissed me.

Then he said, "Do you love me, really love me?" and I said, "Oh God!" and started crying again. Bert left the room and came back a little later with a breakfast tray:

"I called you in sick. Eat something, get some coffee in you and then we can talk."

We talked for hours and Bert, in essence, forgave me. He said he knew from the way I took to sex when we were married that the day would come when I would want to try someone else. He said that he knew I was too highly sexed to be satisfied with one man and that he had always expected that I would stray.

"If it hadn't been the Christmas party it would have been something else, but it would have happened."

He did say that he hadn't thought that I'd take on bunches, but he always knew there was a lover in my future. His only worry had been that whoever I choose might take me away from him. I threw myself at him and hugged him to me.

"Oh no baby, oh God no. I love you and only you and I could never leave you, not ever."

And then he stunned me, "Have your affairs sweetie. Enjoy yourself as much as you want; just promise me that you will always come home to me and stay mine."

That was two years ago. I am still as deeply in love with Bert as ever. It excites me to go home to him after having spent time with Brad, Charlie and any number of other men who have managed to find their way between my legs and give Bert his sloppy seconds. It excites Bert to hear about my escapades and when I'm done he can't keep his hands off of me.

I've offered to bring my lover's home so he can watch from the closet or even participate, but he refuses. He says all he cares about is my happiness and my never leaving him and I have promised him that I am his for life and I meant every word.

Kathy

Sometimes a 'boys night out' can be a pretty life-changing event. I know one of them changed my life – big time!

My 'boys night out' has always been a bone of contention between me and my wife, Madge. But then, it seemed like everything was a bone of contention between us. Truth be told, Madge and I never should have gotten married at all. We mistakenly thought that sexual passion was love and when the fire went out about three years after the wedding, we suddenly found out that we didn't have anything else going for us. The fact that the marriage stumbled along for the next seven years was more of a tribute to our indifference that anything else.

Since I didn't care to stay home and argue with her, I filled my nights with bowling leagues, poker parties and other activities, none of which torqued off Madge more than 'boys night out'. That night, which only took place on the average of one night a month, was when a group of us guys would go out drinking, usually to some titty bar, and then I would stagger home at four in the morning and fall into bed. What pissed Madge off was that she was a light sleeper and when I fell onto the bed, I woke her up and she couldn't fall back to sleep. The end result was that she would be bitchy and irritable and would whine about it all the next day. I could have put an end to it by simply ending the marriage, but I was just too lazy (or too cheap to pay a lawyer) to go to the effort.

Six years ago, a 'boy's night out' changed all that. It changed the lives of several others also, some for the better and some for the worse. As usual, it took place on a Friday night. One of the guys had heard about a new titty bar in Newton, a town about thirty miles from us. We had plenty of titty bars in town and we hardly ever went anyplace else, but that night the boys were feeling adventurous.

The group was short one man that night. Norm's wife had gone back to school and she was working nights as a security guard to earn the money to pay for it. Imagining Kathy as a security guard was a major, major stretch of the imagination and we all tried to picture it until she laughingly broke down and told us that all she had to do was monitor TV screens and call the cops if she saw anything.

Anyway, Norm had to stay home and watch the kids. We made the trip to Newton, got a fairly good table and settled in to enjoy ourselves. We had just ordered our second round when Harry sat straight up in his chair and shouted, "Holy sweet Jesus!"

We all looked at him and he pointed, "Is that who I think it is?" and we looked in the direction he was pointing and my jaw almost hit the floor. On the other side of the room, giving a customer a lap dance was Norm's wife Kathy. We all watched as Kathy did everything except fuck the guy.

Mack said, "You think Norm knows or does he really believe the security guard bullshit?"

None of us could answer that question. Over on the other side of the room, Kathy had finished her lap dance and she went into the back room. Two minutes later, the girl on the stage finished her set, the music changed and Kathy came on the stage and began her dance. We had all seen Kathy in a bikini at pool parties or picnics at the beach and we knew that she had a great body, but we had never seen this Kathy.

She fairly radiated sex as she twisted and turned, dipped and strutted for her audience along the length of the stage and allowed them to tuck bills in her bikini bottoms and the garters she had on her legs. I watched her work her way toward our end of the stage and I wondered what would happen when she saw the five of us sitting there. It was not at all what I expected. I saw the instant recognition in her eyes, but her routine never missed a beat and she never gave any indication that she knew us, not even when Mack tucked a five into her waistband.

When her set was over, she came straight for our table and sat down. As usual, a waitress immediately appeared and we were supposed to buy the dancer a drink. The way it worked was the dancer ordered champagne or some other high dollar drink that that we would pay for and then the waitress would bring the dancer ginger ale or soda water – something non-alcoholic that looked like what the dancer had ordered.

As soon as the formalities were taken care of and the waitress had gone, Kathy said, "You guys going to tell Norm?"

Now Norm is a good friend, but Kathy was a friend too and I had no doubt in my mind that Kathy was dancing here because it paid one hell of a lot more than being a security guard. I couldn't see that it was hurting Norm at all and I didn't see any need to upset the apple cart. But before I could say anything, Harry asked her, "How bad do you want to keep it from him?"

I saw a side of Kathy I'd never seen before. Her eyes went hard and she said in a flat voice, "What are you getting at Harry?"

Harry said, "What are you willing to do to insure that we keep our mouths shut? How far are you willing to go?"

Kathy looked around the table at each of us and then said in a cold flat tone, "I'll do whatever it takes."

"I've watched you parade your body around us for years in bikinis that left nothing to the imagination. I want that body. That's my price."

Kathy looked around the table again, "All of you feel that way?"

When her eyes met mine I said, "Not me. I'll have no part of this" and I saw something in her eyes but I don't know what it was.

She said, "All right. I get off at eleven. I'm not allowed to have anything to do with customers so you will have to meet me away from here."

Harry said, "No problem. I'll get a room at the motel at the other end of town. You can meet us there."

Kathy gave him a hard look and then she got up and walked away. I just sat there and watched as the guys laughed and high-fived each other and talked about their good luck. Mack looked at me:

"What's the matter with you?"

I just shrugged, "You all seem to be forgetting that Norm is our friend and that's Norm's wife you are so gleefully getting ready to blackmail."

He said, "You've seen my wife. Do you honestly think I would pass up a chance at something as nice as Kathy given the chance? Besides, Norm doesn't know she's dancing here and it hasn't hurt him and he won't know about what we are going to do so that won't hurt him either. One other thing to think about; do you really think she would go along with this if all she was doing here was dancing?"

I looked at him, "What's that supposed to mean?"

He snorted. "You saw that lap dance. She did everything but fuck him. What do you want to bet that she gets off at eleven, but dear old Norm doesn't get to see her till three or four? What do you think she is doing with those extra hours? I know what I think and I'm betting that it pays more than dancing."

I remembered Norm telling me that the worst part of Kathy's job was being woke up at three in the morning when she got home. If she did get off at eleven what did she do with those extra hours? Still, she was a friend and what the guys were going to do was wrong.

I said I wasn't going to be a part of it, but to an extent I was. We had all come in my car so I was stuck with staying with the group. I seriously thought of just driving straight home so they couldn't put their plan into play, but then I couldn't be sure that they wouldn't blab to Norm. We pulled in at the motel and Harry went in and got a room and then everyone went inside and waited for Kathy. I went in with the rest of them with the intention of leaving and waiting in the car when Kathy got there. That intention, while noble, didn't last past Kathy's arrival in the room.

There was no bullshit or pleading, she walked to the bed and without saying a word she stripped and lay down. In a voice totally devoid of emotion she said, "Who's first?" and then she just lay there waiting.

The guys all looked at each other. They had been expecting the cheerful, bubbly Kathy that they had always known. Harry finally undressed and got on the bed with her. He pushed her legs apart and she just looked up at him with a blank face as he drove into her. She just lay there and didn't make a sound or move as Harry humped into her. Watching the other guy's watch I knew that Harry was going to be the only one to fuck her.

I saw the guys looking at nervously at each other and I could read their expressions - "What the fuck are we doing here?" Two more minutes and the guys would have gone outside and waited for Harry and we would have all gone on home. But two minutes can be a long time and a lot can happen in that time frame.

Mack got up and was moving toward the door when a low moan came from the bed and we turned and saw her legs come up and wrap around Harry. Seconds later her hands came up and grabbed his ass and her hips started pushing up at him. I looked at the other guys and again I could read their expression - "Hey, this is more like it," and clothes started coming off and on the bed Kathy was hissing at Harry:

"Fuck me you miserable bastard, fuck me."

Harry lasted about five minutes and as he started to pull away from her she grabbed him and tried to pull him back down:

"No, no, no, not yet, I'm almost there, damn you I'm almost there."

Mack grabbed Harry by the shoulders and pulled him off Kathy and shoved him out of the way and he was on her and in her in a flash. Arms and legs came up to grabbed him, "Oh yes oh yes oh yes oh god fuck me fuck me fuck me," and then she gave a loud wail as she came. Mack didn't slow down, he kept ramming his cock into Kathy's pussy and she started moaning again and Mack said, "God is she one hot fuck," and Kathy moaned "Oh yes oh yes oh yes please don't stop please don't stop."

Of course, he eventually had to, but Billy was standing there to immediately take his place. Jeff had been standing there, watching and stroking his cock while waiting his turn, but he got impatient and walked over to the bed and poked his cock at Kathy's mouth. She took it and started sucking on it. All thoughts of my going out to sit in the car were gone. I could not take my eyes off what was happening on the bed.

Billy came and Jeff took his place. Harry took Jeff's place until Jeff came and then he moved to her pussy and Mack moved to her mouth and it just kept on going as one after another they moved from mouth to pussy while Kathy had orgasm after orgasm all the while moaning "oh yes oh yes fuck me fuck me don't stop fucking me."

I happened to look at my watch and saw that it was almost three in the morning. The guys had been fucking Kathy non-stop for almost four hours. "Hey guys," I interrupted the party:

"It's three o'clock. She's got to get home if she wants to stay out of trouble."

There was a lot of grumbling, but the guys started getting dressed. Kathy lay on the bed staring up at the ceiling and I have no idea what she thinking, but she was showing no sign of getting a move on. The guys started leaving and I tossed them my keys and told them to go on without me.

"I'll get her cleaned up and drive her to my place and she can drive home from there."

The door closed behind them and Kathy, still staring up at the ceiling said, "I guess that I let that one get away from me."

I shrugged, "We need to get you into the shower. You can't go home looking like this."

She turned her head and looked at me, "Why didn't you join in. You must have noticed that after the first five minutes I was all too willing."

I shrugged again, "Yeah. But it still wasn't right. Besides, you're my friend and I couldn't do that to you."

She looked me in the eye and said, "But I want you to."

I just looked at her and she said, "I want you to because you are my friend. If you don't the next time you see me, you will look away from me embarrassed by what you saw here tonight. I don't want that. I appreciate that you weren't an asshole like the rest, but I need you to fuck me now if for no other reason so that we will still be able to see each other and talk to each other like we always have. If you fuck me, we are in it together. Am I making sense?"

She reached for my zipper and as she tugged it down all my good intentions were history. She pulled my cock out:

"I'm a little sloppy down there, baby, but no one used my ass tonight. My ass is my gift to you for being so sweet and for being my friend."

When it was over, we showered together which was a mistake. As our hands moved over each other as we washed each other's back, the hands strayed and we didn't get out of that motel room until two fucks and a blowjob later. It was five-thirty when we reached my house and as I climbed out of the car, she reached over and grabbed my arm and pulled me back; she kissed me and said, "I get off every night at eleven Tuesday through Friday, don't be a stranger."

It wasn't supposed to happen, but it did. Word got out about that night and made its way back to Norm. I'm not sure, but I think that it was Mack. I don't have any firm proof, but he showed up one night at the strip club hoping for a repeat performance and Kathy told him that she had paid the price and to get out. I'm betting that he put the word out for spite. Norm confronted Kathy and she told him everything except the part where we made love. The others had gone before what happened between us happened so we were the only two who knew. I felt like a prime asshole when Norm thanked me for being his only true friend.

He and Kathy were divorced and after he had dragged all the other guys through the divorce proceedings, he ended up with the kids and then to spite Kathy more than anything, he moved them across the country. She has visiting rights but it is a little hard to exercise them when the kids are in Delaware and she is in Colorado. Fittingly enough, when the information from Norm's divorce proceedings got out, the wives of the other four hauled them into court and the lawyers stripped them clean. Jeff is the only one who didn't get hurt. He didn't have a pot to piss in and he didn't like his wife anyway.

After my night with Kathy, I started driving over to see her and found out what she did with those hours from eleven to three. The owner of the strip club let her use his office to study and do her homework from school. We went for coffee on several nights and talked and a couple of those nights we ended up at the motel. And one night, I was there and she told me she was sorry, but she had a date that night. The next day she called me and asked me to meet her for coffee.

"You know what I'm doing now, right?"

I shook my head no.

"My date last night was a financial arrangement. Are you surprised at that?"

I admitted that I was.

"That night when all of you had me in that motel room I learned something about myself. I found that I loved what happened to me. I found out how much I loved multiple partners, but at the same time I realized that there was no percentage in giving it away and becoming known as an easy slut. Last night's date was actually a private party for five of the strip clubs partners. I still want to see you and I enjoy your company, but I wanted you to know the kind of girl I've turned out to be. If you stop coming over to watch me dance I'll understand."

That was six years ago. About four months after Norm sued Kathy for divorce, I told my wife that I wanted to end the sham that we were calling a marriage and she was agreeable. We split everything fifty-fifty and I paid the legal expenses. She eventually remarried and she seems to be a lot happier now than she was when we were together.

Two months after my divorce was final and a month after Norm left town, I asked Kathy to move in with me and a year later we got married. She still works at the strip club and she still does private parties. I don't care and in fact it turns me on when she comes home to me after a gangbang. As I'm fucking her, I am reliving the first one in my mind and somehow it keeps me hard even after I cum.

She has asked me several times if I want to go to one of her private gatherings with her, but I've always said no. It was one thing when it was spontaneous as it was the first time, but something else again when it is prearranged and for pay.

"Okay" she said, "How about getting several really good friends, guys who can be discrete, and have a poker party. I'll bet I can make it memorable for them." She grinned, "Maybe we could even make it a weekly thing."

Not a bad idea I thought, not a bad idea at all.

Linda

My deepest, darkest fantasy has always been to watch my wife fuck another man. I wanted to watch her in the throes of passion, clamping her legs around and digging her nails into someone else. I finally got up the courage to mention it to her and she laughed at me:

"Get serious Vern."

Even though she wouldn't admit it, the idea did turn her on. I could tell she was turned on by how wildly she would fuck me after I mentioned it. In a one hundred and eighty-degree turnabout, Linda began to tell me her fantasies. They mostly concerned men with huge cocks, sex with Latinos and gangbangs with blacks. After a couple of weeks of listening to her fantasies, I asked her if she wanted to try them for real. I reminded her of my fantasy and suggested that we could combine our fantasies and each of us would get what we wanted.

"Don't be silly Vern. They are just fantasies."

Whatever they were, the more Linda talked about them, the more sexually charged up she got. Our sex life took a major leap forward and we were having sex six or seven times a week. There were some nights I'd get home from work and find her naked and waiting for me when I walked in the front door. Well, I thought, I may not be getting my fantasy, but I'll damn sure take all the sex that talking about the fantasy brings me.

Then I began to suspect that Linda was having an affair. She was never home when I called during the day or if she was, she wouldn't answer the phone. Her wardrobe, especially as far as sexy lingerie was concerned, grew at a rapid rate and I knew for sure that a lot of it she never wore for me. What I didn't understand was why if she was having an affair, she was hiding it from me. She had to know that she would have had my complete approval.

I'd been mentioning my desire to see her with another man for quite some time, but all she did was to continue to relate her fantasies to me at night when we were in bed. I began to think that what she was relating were not actual fantasies, but what she had been actually doing with her lover or lovers.

One night, I got some confirmation of my theory. Linda was really hot when I got home from work that night and she met me at the front door wearing only high heels and with a martini in her hand for me. We went straight up to the bedroom and she asked me to eat her pussy. When I went down on her, I found that she was sopping wet. One of Linda's favorite fantasies was for me to eat her pussy after she had been fucked by someone else and she was relating that fantasy to me as I licked and sucked on her pussy. I'd eaten her a hundred times, but something was different this time; I was certain that I was cleaning up after another man and I told Linda that.

"Well, what if it's true. You always said you wanted me to fuck another man. Is it making you horny to know you are sucking up another man's leavings?"

I told her that it was and she said, "Then you might as well know that he left twenty minutes before you got home."

I climbed on top of her and drove my cock into her. When I was finally wiped out two hours later, Linda confessed that it wasn't the first time I'd gotten sloppy seconds from her. I asked why, knowing what my fantasy has always been, she had been hiding her affair from me. She told me that she just could not bring herself to believe that any man could get a kick out of knowing that his wife was out fucking around.

"I know you say you want it, but I also knew that the odds were good that if I did it and it wasn't near the kick you thought it would be you might call me a whore, a slut, an unfaithful bitch and go for a divorce."

I told her that now she knew better and I hoped she wouldn't hide things from me anymore.

She gave me a long look and said, "Are you absolutely sure that this turns you on?"

I assured her that it did and she said, "He hasn't had my ass yet. Would it turn you on knowing that the next time I see him he's going to fuck my butt?"

I pushed her back down on the bed and fucked her again.

No matter how much I begged and pleased, Linda wouldn't tell me who her lover was. I suspected that it was someone we knew and she was afraid I would be pissed off when I found out. I spent the next six months looking closely at everyone I knew to see if they were acting differently around me, but I was never able to come up with a suspect. Whoever it was who was pulling down her panties was nailing her four and five times a week and then Linda would come home and try to fuck me to death. She got a particular charge out of sitting on my face after her lover had come in her and asking me to clean her out.

While I did she would talk to me. "Do you like it honey? Do you love the taste of my lover? I told him you suck his juices out of me and he laughed and said that he would see to it you got plenty. He fucked me five times today honey – five loads of cum just for you."

I asked her if he ate her after I fucked her and she said, "Oh no, he's not that kind of guy," which made me wonder just what kind of guy she thought that made me. I drew the line on the day she gave him her ass. I absolutely refused to clean her even though she begged me. We had our first major argument over her affair that day. She indicated that if I wouldn't clean her ass, she might not feel like making love that night and I told her that if that was the case she could end her affair or get her ass out of the house.

Then she got all weepy and said that I had told her that I was all right with her fucking around on me. I told her that I was, but that my attitude would change in a heartbeat if she was going to try and use sex as a weapon. Then I reminded her how generous I was being in letting her do her thing while she still was denying me mine by not letting me watch. Then she said she wanted to, but her lover was adamant that I never find out who he was, so I said that maybe what she needed to do then was dump him and get someone else.

"Oh baby, why are we arguing over this when we could be upstairs in bed?" She stretched out her hand to me, "Come on baby, let's go to bed so I can show you how much I need you."

Her putting an abrupt end to our discussion was the first time her affair really bothered me because it indicated to me reluctance on her part to break with this specific person; it pointed to a real emotional attachment to someone other than me. I wasn't really sure that I cared for that.

Curiosity finally got the best of me and I made a determined effort to find out who this person was that Linda couldn't bear to give up and while I wasn't able to find out who it was, I did narrow the field. I had some comp time coming at work and I arranged to take some of it off. I didn't tell Linda I was taking off work and every morning for five days, I left the house at the regular time and then parked where I could watch the house. When Linda left the house I followed her.

For the five days, I was off nothing at all happened. No one came to the house and Linda never went anywhere where she could have met her lover. That told me one of two things: her lover took a vacation or a business trip at the particular time I decided to play detective, and how likely was that, or her lover worked were I did and when he asked Linda what we were going to do on my time off and she said, "Say what?" and the two of them figured out what I was up to. The one thing

I did find out though was how edgy Linda got when she was down to getting sex from only me.

Then one day, I accidentally stumbled onto who it was. It was a Saturday and Linda had gone shopping. I was a little behind on a project at work so for the first time in over a year, I went into the office on a weekend. There were three cars in the parking lot, my boss's car, the security guard's car and Linda's car. I could see the security guard sitting at the desk in the lobby and he was alone – Linda was fucking my boss!

No wonder he didn't want me to know who he was. How had they gotten together? How had they started the affair? A far as I knew, Jason had only met Linda once, two years ago at the company picnic, but their affair had only been going on now for about nine months – or had it been going on much longer and I had been brain dead and been getting sloppy seconds a lot longer than I thought? I was both embarrassed and aroused at the thought of Jason fucking my wife. I was going to have to be very careful from now on to keep the two of them from knowing that I now knew.

I could not see any positive benefit from their knowing that I was aware, but I could see plenty of negatives, especially on the job. If Jason knew that I knew he was fucking my wife, the office dynamic could be altered in ways that neither of us would care for and the solution to the problem would inevitably be my being gone from the company. On the other hand, if I could get the two of them to bring me in on the relationship I could see all kinds of positives. Without letting on that I knew who her lover was, I began to drop hints that I would like to try a threesome with Linda and her lover. Linda told me that the thought of doing two men at the same time excited her, but she didn't think her lover would go for it.

"I already told you he doesn't want you to know who he is."

I asked her to at least mention it to him and two days later she told me that he was willing to see that she got the experience, but not with me.

Last Tuesday night when I got home from work, Linda told me that she had been fucked by two men that afternoon.

"They both fucked me three times honey and I loved it. Are you going to eat me now?"

I am really turned on by the thought that my wife is so sexual that it takes more than one man to satisfy her and I love eating her and then fucking her after she has enjoyed another cock. Linda has been getting fucked almost daily for the last couple of months so she is used to getting a steady supply of cock.

Jason is going to Europe for three weeks and I'm betting that by the end of the first week he is gone, Linda will be starving for cock. I'm planning on having several friends over for cards and we will see what happens. I just might finally get my fantasy.

Mandy

We were sitting at the table and I was pulling on a longneck while she was sipping her vodka tonic and watching the dance the floor. Actually, she wasn't watching the dance floor as much as she was watching one of the dancers. He was a lean, tall man of about thirty and he had become Amanda's favorite dance partner since I broke my foot. There was a mutual attraction between the two of them and everybody at the Silver Palace, including me, knew that they would eventually end up in bed together. Well, almost everybody. Amanda didn't know it, and while Toby might have hoped for it he certainly never expected that it would happen.

Amanda and I had been coming to the Silver Palace at least twice a month for the past fifteen years. Mandy loved to dance and while I wasn't all that keen on it, I was willing to do whatever it took to keep her happy. Mandy came along late in my life and I was still amazed that the raven haired beauty had wanted me enough to chase me until I finally caved in and asked her to marry me. Everyone, and I do mean everyone, had warned us not to get married and I knew that they were right, but Mandy owned me by then and I would do anything that she wanted. I warned her several time myself that the twenty years between us in age was going to be a major problem later on.

"Bullshit! You either love me or you don't. If you love me now you will still love me later and that's all that counts," she said instead.

She had been right about that part at least, I did love her then and I loved her as much if not more now. But the naysayers had been right too and now I was in the position that I'd known I would be in, but hadn't been able to convince Mandy of. I was sixty-five to her forty-five and I couldn't get it up anymore without the help of a little blue pill, and the pill didn't always work. To make matters worse, Mandy was in her sexual prime and even though she would not admit it she was suffering from a lack of sex.

After thinking long and hard on the situation, I finally sat down with her and told her that it wasn't fair of me to keep her tied down at this point in her life and I offered to let her go free. She laughed at me and told me I wasn't going to get rid of her that easy.

"I knew this day would possibly come, but I loved you enough to marry you anyway. So stop being an asshole and trying to get rid of me."

A couple of months went by and I noticed that about twice a week she would get cranky and irritable and I knew what the problem was, so I sat down with her again and told her that she needed to take care of the problem.

"You are not cheating on me sweetheart, not if you have my permission and blessing. Do what you have to do to take the edge off. I'm not going to stop loving you and maybe, just maybe, you will stop being such a bear to be around."

She kissed me and thanked me for loving her enough to trust her with something like that:

"But I can't do it baby, I belong to you, heart and soul."

And now, I'd let her down again. Couldn't make love to her and now I couldn't even do her next favorite thing – dance. I'd broken a foot trying to break a horse and I'd been walking around in a cast for a month now. I'd been bringing her to the Silver Palace every weekend since I'd broken my foot so she could at least dance. There was no lack of partners and she would be on the floor for most of the night.

It didn't seem to matter who she was with on a tush-push or other line dance, or who she did the western swing with, but I noticed that she always managed to do the slow ones with Toby, especially the slow ones where they could get close. And I noticed the times she left the bar with Toby to get some fresh air. They were never gone long enough to do anything and somehow this saddened me. When we got home, she would toss and turn and I would lay there on my back staring up at the ceiling and curse the fact that I couldn't help her.

I took another pull on my long-neck and looked at Mandy watching the dance floor and then I said, "Mandy, go ahead and do it. You know you want to and you know it's all right with me. Will you please do it? If not for yourself, do it for me. It's killing me to see you this way."

She turned and smiled at me, "Sorry baby. You're right, I do want to, but even though you say you won't care there is always the possibility that once it happens you will find out that you really did care. I not willing to risk what I have in you on anything less than a sure thing and that animal just doesn't exist."

On the drive home that night, I thought about what she'd said and as I lay on the bed next to her as she tossed and turned, I thought about it some more.

The next morning, I went out and made some arrangements and then I called Toby and told him I had to go away for a few days and I asked him if I could hire him to take care of the stock while I was gone.

"It's a little too much for Mandy to do all by herself."

He said he would be glad to help out and then I went and broke the news to Mandy. She just looked at me and asked, "What are you doing?"

I smiled at her and said, "I'm giving you the chance to do what you really want to do without me being around. If you don't do it, so be it, but in the back of my mind I'll always believe that you did and my attitude toward you will be the same as if you did and I knew about it.

I'll be gone four days. Have fun and remember that I love you and always will."

Then I went and packed what I needed and loaded it in the back of my pickup. Toby showed up and I took him down and showed him the bunkhouse and told him what needed doing. Then I went and kissed Mandy goodbye, got in my truck and drove off. I really didn't have any place that I needed to be, but I had to give Mandy a chance so I faked the trip. I actually drove about three-quarters of a mile up into the hills and settled into a hide that I'd set up earlier. I've been a hunter all my life and patience is something that a hunter learns early on. I got out my field glasses and settled in to watch.

I watched Mandy hang out the laundry and Toby feed and water the horses. That evening, I watched as they ate their supper on the screened in porch, sat and talked for a while, and then watched as Toby made the trip to the bunkhouse. And I was watching two hours later as Mandy, in the light of the full moon, walked down to the bunkhouse. I watched for another hour and when she didn't come out I smiled and crawled into my sleeping bag. I was behind the glasses the next morning when a naked Mandy walked from the bunkhouse to the main house. Five minutes later Toby, clad only in Levi's, followed her to the house. I watched as Mandy, still naked, served Toby his breakfast on the back porch and when they finished eating she took him by the hand and led him into the house. I gave them ten minutes and then I took out my cell phone and called the house.

Mandy answered on the fifth ring and after the hellos were out of the way I said, "Behaving yourself?"

She said, "You are an evil man, but I love you anyway. No, I am not behaving myself. I had to stop sucking his cock to answer this phone and he's waiting for me to come back to the bedroom and pick up where I left off. I sure hope you meant what you said about not caring because by the time you get back I'm liable to be Toby's slut. When you set this up did you realize that he has a cock the size of a horses? The stock might not get taken care of baby because I might never let him leave the bedroom until you get back. I'll talk to you later baby. I need to get back to him before he loses that beautiful hard on. I love you baby, and baby – thank you."

I had a piece of news to share with her, but she hung up before I could say another word. I had the first hard on in over a year that hadn't required Viagra and I wondered what that meant. I broke camp and headed for Helena where I spent the next three days visiting friends.

Five miles from the house, I pulled over to the side of the road and called the house to let Mandy know I was almost there just in case she needed time to do whatever. Toby was watering the horses when I got there and Mandy was sitting on the front porch watching him. I pulled into the yard and she came running up to me, threw her arms around me and gave me a long lingering kiss. She stepped back and looked into my eyes.

"Are we all right baby?"

I smiled at her and said, "We can talk about it when we are alone, but yes, we are all right."

I paid Toby for his help and he told me I could call him anytime I needed help. Mandy had the good grace to blush at that and Toby got into his pickup and left. Mandy and I walked into the house hand in hand.

"Before you tell me everything, and I do want to know everything I have something to say. When I called you that first day and you told me what was happening I got a hard on just listening and knowing that you were going to go back to him. So don't spare me the details. I want to see if it will happen again."

Mandy told me in detail everything that had happened. It had been four days of near non-stop sex and to Toby's credit, he did tear himself away from Mandy long enough to do the chores I had hired him to do. But to my disappointment, and Mandy's, no hard on was produced by her story.

"Maybe it happened because while you were talking to me it was actually going on."

I thought about it and saw that she could be right, "When are you going to see him again?"

Her face clouded over and she said, "I'm not."

I asked her why and she it was one thing when I was not around, but she didn't think she could leave me sitting at home, go out and get laid, and then return to me.

"Not even if it will give me a hard on? You were the one who told me you would be his slut by the time I got back. Was that just bullshit, or are you his slut?"

She looked away and said, "Yes, I was a slut for that huge cock of his. An absolute total slut and I let him do whatever he wanted to me, but you're home now."

I was silent for a moment or two and then said, "Basically you are telling me that if I leave home for two or three days a week he can fuck you silly while I'm gone, but not at any other time?"

"All right god damn it, I want him!"

I smiled and said, "Good. Here is what we will do."

The next morning, she called Toby and arranged to meet him that night. She called me on her cell phone as soon as she pulled up in front of Toby's rented room. I gave her ten minutes and then I called her,

"Hello?"

"Having fun?"

"Oh god yes baby, I miss you."

"Is he in you?"

"Yes."

"Did you suck his cock first?"

"Yes I did."

"Will you do it again tonight?"

"Yes baby, you know I will."

"Good. Just so you know; I have a rock hard cock right now. Take your time, enjoy yourself, and then hurry home."

Mandy came home two hours later, but the hard on was long gone.

"Oh baby" Mandy cried, "I hurried honey, honestly, I did." I shrugged my shoulders,

"Not you, fault sweetie. If you had left as soon as I hung up you still wouldn't have made it in time. It stayed up for fifteen or twenty minutes and then it was gone."

She gave me a long thoughtful look, "Twenty minutes, huh?"

She moaned, groaned and cried. She twisted and turned and thrashed around on the bed and I watched from the closet as Toby buried his huge cock in Mandy's hot, wet pussy. They had been at it for over an hour and showed no signs of slowing down. When Toby had arrived, Mandy had not wasted any time on small talk or foreplay. She had pulled him into the bedroom, stripped him, pushed him back on the bed and then had gone down on him.

Every once in a while, she would look over at the closet where she knew I was standing with my eyes glued to her and when Toby came in her mouth I saw cum squirt out of its corners. She gulped and swallowed and kept his cock in her mouth until he was hard again and then she had climbed on the bed and opened her legs for him.

He buried his cock in her and within minutes she had forgotten I was even there as Toby brought her to orgasm after orgasm. When I finally reached the point where I couldn't stand it anymore, I took out my cell phone and hit the preset for my home phone. It took seven rings before Mandy came out of her sexually induced trance and answered it. I didn't say a word, but Mandy knew the script, "Yes baby, I'll be waiting for you," and she hung up the phone. "You have to go lover, he's on his way home."

Toby got off the bed, "Damn, I wasn't near ready."

Mandy said, "Sorry lover, I'll try to make it up to you next time. I'll call you when I know I'll be able to see you again."

The front door hadn't fully closed and I was out of the closet and on Mandy with a genuine, bona fide hard dick and we made love for almost half an hour before I came. That was the first time and we managed to do it two or three times a week for the next few months.

Then Toby started to get a little too possessive and Mandy was forced to dump him. It was back to trying Viagra again and in the next month or so the little blue pill only got me up on the average of once a week. I missed Toby, oh god did I ever miss him.

We were at the Silver Palace one night about two months after Mandy had sent Toby packing. Mandy had been out on the dance floor for about twenty minutes and was having a good time. My foot was out of the cast now, but still a little too tender for anything but a slow two-step. She came back to the table and said, "I didn't realize that Toby was an asshole, but he was and maybe it is a good thing."

I looked at her and waited for the explanation.

"He apparently told Todd that I was a great piece of ass and now Todd wants to find out if it's true."

I still didn't know what she was getting at and she smiled at me, "You think if I was to get him out to the truck you could manage to be somewhere close by?"

I was and when Todd was through and had gone back inside, I was next in line. Toby told a lot of guys about Mandy and soon we were at the Silver Palace every Friday and Saturday night where Mandy managed to get in quite a bit of seat time in the truck.

One night, as she was busy sucking Todd's cock, another guy came out and after a quick look to where she knew I was, she took on both of them and from there it just seemed to escalate. Mandy spends so much time on the truck seat that I get a little impatient waiting my turn.

Just last night at the Palace, I had to wait until seven guys finished with her. Mandy isn't complaining and as long as her being a slut makes my dick hard, I won't either.

Nancy

Nancy and I have been married for a bit more than twenty years, and for nineteen of those years, my biggest fantasy has been to see her with another man. Nancy and I have always been open and honest with each other so she has always known about my desire to watch her. It really didn't surprise me when she said no, but her 'no' didn't stop my continuing to fantasize about it off and on over the years.

Nancy and I both work and her job requires some travel while mine doesn't. Nancy was in New York and I was home watching the Raven's play the Bronco's on Monday Night Football when the phone rang. I had been expecting Nancy to call so I hit the mute button on the TV and picked up the cordless. We exchanged hellos, made small talk for a minute or so and I got the feeling that something was bothering her.

"What's the matter sweetie?"

There was a hesitation on the other end and then she said, "We have a problem honey and I don't quite know how to talk about it. I thought that I would wait until I got home so I could talk to you face to face, but if I don't get it out of my system I'm not going to be able to sleep tonight or even function on the job tomorrow. I guess that the best way is to just say it. I got screwed by another man today."

I wasn't sure that I'd heard her right, "You what?"

"I'm sorry honey. I didn't really want to do it, but I felt that I had no choice."

I was silent, stunned by what she had said.

"Honey, are you still there?"

"Yes sweetie, I'm still here. What happened?"

Nancy had gotten out of a meeting at three and had gone back to the hotel to take a shower and dress for a cocktail party that was to be held that evening. She got in the elevator and the door had started to close and someone had hollered

"Hold the elevator please."

Nancy had stopped the elevator door from closing and a man had hurried into the elevator and thanked her for holding it for him.

"These elevators are notoriously slow and I need to get to my room, grab some papers and get back to a meeting."

Nancy pushed the button for eighteen and the man had said, "Sixteen for me please."

The elevator had just passed the tenth floor when the elevator shuddered and came to a stop between the tenth and eleventh floors. Nancy waited a minute or so and when nothing happened she pushed the emergency button and a bell started ringing. Another minute passed by and then the man start asking, "What's happening, what's going on, they need to get us out of here. They need to get us out of here now. Make them do something."

Just then a voice came over the speaker just below the floor button panel and said that they were aware of the problem, but that it was going to be at least fifteen or twenty minutes before the elevator repairman would get there with the relay that they needed. As soon as the man with Nancy heard that he started yelling.

"No, no, you have to get us out of here now, right now."

Nancy had looked at him and he had a panicky look on his face and his face was covered with sweat. As the minutes passed by, the man seemed to get progressively worse. His body was shaking uncontrollably and he kept moaning.

"Get me out of here, get me out of here."

He started beating on the walls of the elevator and shouting and a minute or so later he took his briefcase and began to swing it wildly about, bashing it into the walls trying to break his way out. Nancy began to fear for her safety. Several times his flailing briefcase almost hit her.

"I had to do something to calm him down, to take his mind off the situation. I tried talking to him, but that didn't work so I hollered at him to shut up and told him he was making me crazy and he either didn't hear me or he ignored me. I was trying to think of something else when his briefcase hit my shoulder and I dropped to my knees so I'd be under his swings. I was staring right at his crotch and for some reason that gave me the idea."

While he kept beating on the walls with his briefcase, Nancy had undone his belt, pulled down his zipper and then had pulled down his pants. She had taken the man's cock in her hand and had started stroking him and that slowed him down a little but he didn't stop. She had leaned forward and had taken his cock in her mouth and started to suck on him. It took him a minute to realize what was happening, but soon the wild swinging at the walls stopped, he dropped his briefcase and both of his hands had gone to the back of Nancy's head. He was still moaning "Get me out, get me out" but he had stopped being violent.

"I did all the things that you told me you liked; I played with his balls, teased his ass with my fingers and used my tongue as much as possible. I was concentrating on trying to keep him calm and quiet and not too much on anything else so when he came I had him deep in my throat and I had to gulp and swallow to keep his stuff from getting all over my dress. His dick was just starting to go soft when the loud speaker said that the part they needed had just arrived and they would need another ten minutes before they would be able to get us out.

"I felt the man tense up and I knew I had to keep him occupied or he was going to get wild on me again so I shoved a finger up his ass and kept on licking and sucking on him and he began to get hard again. My jaw was starting to ache and I knew I couldn't keep sucking him for another ten minutes so I did the only other thing I could think of. I took off my panties, turned and leaned against the wall and told him to fuck me. I stood there, legs spread wide, leaning against the wall and let him take me from behind.

"Until then I had been doing what I thought I needed to do to keep myself from getting hurt, not that he would have done it on purpose, but when he slid his cock into me things changed. I started to get hot and I began to push back at him and asking him to fuck me harder, to make me cum. His hands came around to the front of me and he started to play with my breasts so I opened the front of my dress and pushed down my bra so he could get his hands on them. I felt so damned deliciously wicked to be leaning against a wall while a man whose name I didn't even know and whom I'd never seen before fucked me from behind like some slut off the street. I had two orgasms before he shot his cum in me, but I didn't want to stop.

"I felt him going soft in me so I pulled away from him and went back down on my knees and started sucking him again. I licked and sucked and did my best to get him hard again so he could fuck me some more. It took me two minutes and I had him up again and then I jumped up and leaned against the wall again and begged him to hurry up and put it in me. I felt like a twenty dollar street whore leaning against an alley wall while my john was taking me from behind, but just as he pushed into me the elevator gave a sudden lurch and we both started to scramble and get our clothes on and get presentable.

"The elevator went down to the lobby and the manager and some of his staff was waiting for us. The manager apologized profusely for the inconvenience, took our names and room numbers and told us our stay would be on the house. As I went to get back on the elevator, I noticed a drop of cum on the toe of one of my high heels and I prayed that no one else had seen it. The man who had been in the elevator with me wouldn't get back in – he took the stairs up to his room."

"I was still hotter than hell when I got to my room so I headed straight for the bathroom and grabbed my hairbrush and I was lying on the bed using it as a dildo when someone knocked on the door. I got up and straightened my dress and answered the door and when I opened it I found the man from the elevator standing there. He started to say something, but I reached out, grabbed him and pulled him into the room, drug him over to the bed and practically raped the poor man. He fucked me twice before I cooled down enough to leave him alone. He had come to my room to apologize for his behavior. He is claustrophobic and he can handle it for short periods of time, but he came totally unglued when he heard how long we were going to be stuck. He thanked me for helping him get through the ordeal and then he asked me if he could buy me dinner as a way of saying thanks. After dinner, I went with him to his room and I let him fuck me again. Honey, I'm sorry."

I had sat quietly as I beat my meat while listening to her describe what had happened and trying to picture it in my mind.

"You don't need to apologize to me sweetie. You did what you had to do."

There was silence on the other end of the line for a moment or two and then Nancy said:

"No honey, I'm not sorry that I did it in the elevator, or that we did it again in my room and still again in his room. What I'm sorry about is that you didn't get to see it. I know it's what you have always wanted and it happened and you weren't there."

She wasn't near as sorry about it as I was. As it was I would probably beat my meat raw before she got home and I could get my hands on her.

"You know I'm going to be all over you when you get home, don't you?"

"You might have more on your hands than you can handle. The more he fucked me the hornier I got and the more I wanted to fuck."

"Are you going to see him again?"

"I'm looking at him right now. I'm still in his room and I'm using his phone. He's sleeping, but I'm stroking his cock with my right hand while holding the phone in my left. If I can get him up I'm going to fuck him again and I'll probably spend the rest of the night here and fuck him again in the morning. Don't hate me honey. I promise you I'll do it again when I get home so you can be there to watch, okay?"

I told her it would be okay and then I told her that I loved her and when she hung up I got up and went looking for something to clean up the mess I'd just made.

Hetty

Hetty had been a cock teaser for as long as I had known her and that had been since the third grade. As she grew too old to play 'doctor' and as her body blossomed, she took to wearing short skirts, tight sweaters, low cut blouses and whatever else it took to titillate the boys. As a teen, she dated a lot and a lot of guys had some pretty hot times with Hetty, but she always stopped short and sent her dates home with a case of blue balls. You would think that with that reputation the boys would avoid her like the plague, but Hetty had that certain something that always kept them coming back.

In our senior year, one of Hetty's girlfriends told her brother that Hetty had said that she planned to give up her virginity on the night of the Senior Prom. The word got out and the competition started to see who would be her date. The long list of her suitors included almost all of the most popular guys in school (much to the annoyance of their regular girlfriends) and I stood off to the side and watched to see whom she would pick.

Why was I watching and not trying to be the lucky guy? Well, I was just one of the many run of the mill guys who were always part of the background in school. I was a so-so student, wasn't good enough to be first string in any of the sports I went out for, didn't belong to any of the clubs or take part in any after school activities. I was the guy that everybody recognized and nodded hello to, but whose name they couldn't remember. Also, I had pretty low self-esteem and I couldn't see that I had a chance against all the popular guys.

It was two weeks from prom night and Hetty still hadn't made a choice. I was sitting outside on the school steps at lunchtime when Hetty walked up and sat down beside me.

"Hi."

"Hi yourself. What's up?"

"You going to the prom?"

"Probably."

"Who is your date?"

"Don't know. Haven't asked anyone yet."

"Does that mean I might have a chance?"

"What?"

"Does that mean that I might have a chance that you will ask me."

I turned and stared at her. Here was Hetty basically asking me to be her prom date and if the rumors were true, she was also asking me to take her cherry. I was incredulous, but eventually I managed to get my shit together and find my voice.

"Would you like to go to the prom with me?"

"I thought you would never ask. Yes, I would."

All of a sudden, I became the most looked-at guy at school. Girls were looking at me and whispering among themselves and guys were looking at me with "What's so special about him" looks on their faces. The prom came and things were great right up to the time I tried to put the moves on Hetty. We had been making out pretty hot and heavy and I had gotten her bra off and had my hands on her tits and she had not resisted one bit. I unzipped myself and took out my cock and tried to put Hetty's hand on it and she shot me down.

"I'm sorry Brian. I know what you were expecting, but it isn't going to happen. I don't know where that rumor came from, but it isn't true. I'm not giving up my virginity until I get married and I'm not getting married until I finish college. I picked you to be my date for the prom because I know you are a nice guy and will take no for an answer."

To say I was crushed would be an understatement. Here, I had thought that I was something special when all it was was that I was a nice guy and could be counted to take a no and live with it.

I was a little bitter over being used by Hetty so I did some not so nice things where she was concerned. Guys I knew would ask me how it was taking Hetty's cherry and I would just smile and say, "Hey, a gentleman doesn't talk about things like that."

I left everyone who talked to me with the impression that even though I wasn't going to talk about it I'd had a great time. Word got back to Hetty and she told a few of her friends that it was bullshit and when it came back around to me that she had denied it, I just smiled and said, "A gentleman never calls a lady a liar."

The more Hetty protested her innocence and denied that anything had happened, the more I smiled and shrugged my shoulders, "If the lady says it isn't true then it must not be true. Hetty wouldn't lie, now would she?"

The incident did spark some interest in me by the other girls at school and until I graduated, I never lacked for a date on the weekends and I had a pretty impressive list of conquests to my credit before I went off to college. Hetty and I both went off to college – different ones – and I did not see her again until two months after I had graduated with my BS in Business Management. We ran into each other while out beating the bushes looking for jobs. We had lunch together several times, something clicked and we started dating.

Hetty was still a tease. When she found a job, she dressed to tease at work. When we went out, she dressed to attract attention and she necked with me to the point of explosion, but whenever I tried to go the distance she would push me away, "You know the rule Brian. Nothing until I get married." I finally got around to proposing, she accepted and we got married.

Hetty was indeed a virgin when we got married and went to bed for the first time, but she was determined to make up for lost time. Hetty wanted to try everything she had ever heard or read about and she wanted to try it often. I had somewhat expected that sex as newlyweds would be frequent and intense, but I wasn't prepared for Hetty's newfound sexual appetite. It was every night, twice and sometimes three times and then again in the morning before getting up. Hetty was as close to being a nymphomaniac as you could get and it was all I could do to keep up. There was one thing that marriage didn't change – Hetty was still a tease.

When she went to work, when we went out or when we had company over Hetty dressed to tease. She loved to bend over and 'accidentally' give guys a look down her blouse or up her skirt. If she danced with someone he could count on Hetty being plastered to him. She never stopped anybody from stealing a kiss or copping a feel or thinking he could get her in the sack – at least not until the very last minute.

At first, her behavior pissed me off. It was one thing when she was single, but something else now that she was a married woman. We had some pretty nasty fights there for a while when I'd get upset over her letting some guy paw her, but she would always shrug it off with, "So what baby? All it does is get me hotter than hell and then you get to cool me down."

"Yeah," I said, "Right up until the time you do it with the wrong guy and he doesn't take no for an answer."

"Don't you worry baby, I can handle myself."

~~***~~

Over the years, I mellowed out and just let her do her thing without fussing over it, but in retrospect I probably should have put my foot down and stopped it. Everybody has a breaking point and sooner or later, Hetty was going to take things just one step too far.

Although neither Hetty nor I knew it at the time, her company picnic was the last straw for several of the men she worked with. Hetty attended wearing a skimpy halter-top without a bra and a pair of "Daisy Duke" shorts and I'm sure that there wasn't a soft dick at the park. Since it was her company picnic, I was the designated driver and that freed Hetty up to hit the beer keg without worries.

I'm not much of a games person, but when Hetty gets a snootfull, she gets real playful. All of the single guys (and a few of the married ones) worked at getting her to be their partner in various events, like the wheelbarrow race, the three legged race and the balloon race. The wheelbarrow race was the first event that Hetty took part in and halfway through the race, her left tit fell out of her halter top as she was trying to run on her hands. She told her partner not to stop and she finished the race with the tit hanging down and swaying. She got more than a few nasty looks from the wives and mothers there, but I can tell you that none of the men (me excepted) seemed to mind in the least bit.

Next was the three-legged race. There was a small hill leading down to the finish line and Hetty and her partner tripped coming down it and they ended up rolling down the hill with their arms wrapped around each other. They didn't break apart as soon as they stopped rolling and from where I was standing, I could see that they were kissing and the guy was humping Hetty's leg. It only lasted a few seconds, but it did happen.

In the balloon race, two people put a water-filled balloon between them, chest to chest or belly to belly, and raced from the start line to the finished line without breaking or dropping the balloon. Hetty and her partner didn't get fifteen feet from the start line before their balloon broke soaking Hetty's halter-top, which had the same effect as if she had been in a wet tee shirt contest. Hetty didn't try to dry off or to go to the car and get another top – she just walked around and let the men look at her tits through the wet halter-top.

About an hour before the picnic was over, just as it was turning dark, I saw Hetty and a man walk off to a stand of trees. The trees blocked whatever was going on, but ten minutes passed by before Hetty came out from behind the trees alone. A few minutes later, the guy came into view walking very gingerly – the same way I walked the last time I was kicked in the balls. On the way home, I asked Hetty what had happened, "He got fresh and I had to knee him in the balls to turn him off."

"What were you doing going behind the trees with him in the first place?"

"Nothing. We were just walking and talking."

Yeah, right I thought. Walking, talking, leading him on and teasing him.

We didn't know it at the time but Hetty had finally gone too far and with the wrong guy.

~~***~~

It was the night of her company Christmas party and Hetty was going to it alone. I had fallen down on a patch of ice and twisted my ankle rather badly. To make matters worse, I seemed to be coming down with the flu. I wasn't really keen on the idea of her going without me, but she pooh-poohed my concern, "I'm a big girl now Brian. I can look out for myself."

I was lying on the bed watching her put on her nylons and garter belt and then slipping into a simple black mini cocktail dress. She finished off the outfit with a single strand of pearls and then she stepped into a pair of black CFMs with four-inch heels. She did a full turn in front of me and asked, "How do I look?" Before I could answer she giggled and said, "I can see that you like," and sure enough my cock was standing straight up.

"Poor baby, I can't leave you like that," and she knelt next to the bed and gave me a blowjob. Hetty has a magic mouth and it didn't take her long to get me off. She surprised me when I came by not swallowing like she usually did. Instead, she swished it around in her mouth like mouthwash before swallowing. She saw my curious look and giggled, "I might want to let a few guys kiss me under the mistletoe. Think they'll notice the taste?"

Hetty left and I swallowed a bunch of medicine and went to sleep. I woke up in the middle of the night needing to go to the bathroom. The clock said 3:27 and Hetty wasn't in bed with me. I took my whiz and then walked through the house to see if Hetty was home – she wasn't. I called the hotel where the party had been held and was told that the last of the partygoers had gone and only the cleaning crew was in the ballroom. I was a little worried, but I managed to talk myself into waiting a while longer before getting in a panic. There were some possible reasons for her not being home. She could have stopped for an early breakfast like we used to do when we closed down the bars. They may have been under a deadline to get out of the ballroom and had taken the party somewhere else. I took another dose of Ny-Quill and fell back asleep.

The phone woke me up at 7:15 and it was Hetty. "Did I wake you?"

I mumbled that she had.

"I'm sorry honey. I didn't call you last night because I didn't want to wake you up, but I thought you would be up by now and I didn't want you to worry because I'm not there. I had way too much to drink last night and the boss's wife took my keys away from me and made me check into a room. I'm still a little woozy so I'm going to take a shower and have some breakfast before I head home. Will you be okay until I get there?"

I assured her that I could hang on until she could get home. Things changed after that night, but I was so busy wrapped up in my own problems at work that I didn't notice for a couple of weeks. Hetty started working late two and three nights a week. On some mornings, she left for work two hours earlier than she had been and three times she told me she had to work Saturdays to help with an inventory. It was the last, the inventory that finally got my attention. I have been involved in doing inventories and you do not do them one day a week for three weeks. You gear up to do them and then you do them all at one time even if it takes you two or three days.

Then I began to get the feeling that she was nervous whenever she came home from working late. Our sex life changed and began to drop in frequency, although not in intensity, and I began to wonder what was wrong. It hadn't occurred to me that these were some of the signs that indicated the possibility of an unfaithful wife. It didn't occur to me until I picked up a pair of cum soaked panties from the bathroom floor.

Hetty had come home from working late and had undressed to take a shower. I had gone into the bathroom to use the toilet and I saw Hetty's panties lying on the floor next to the dirty clothesbasket. She must have tossed her dirty clothes in the basket and the panties had missed and fallen to the floor. I picked them up to drop them into the basket, but I found that they were soaking wet. Not watery wet, but thick wet if you know what I mean. I looked at what I had in my hand and I knew immediately what it was and to be that wet it had to be fairly fresh. I dropped them back onto the floor and went ahead and sat down on the toilet, did my business and waited for Hetty to come out of the shower.

The shower water stopped running and then the door opened and Hetty came out and reached for a towel. I sat there on the pot and watched her dry herself and then I pointed at the panties and said, "You missed."

"Honestly Brian, would it have killed you to pick them up and drop them in the hamper?"

"I did pick them up Hetty, but I didn't like the way they felt so I dropped them."

Hetty bent down to pick them up and as soon as they were in her hand her face lost its color, "Oh God, oh dear God."

"Why God? You think he can help you get out of this?"

She looked at me, face stricken, said "Oh God" once again and then ran from the room. I got off the toilet and followed her and found that she had gone into the spare bedroom and locked the door behind her. I was angry, but not so angry as to go and kick the door down. She had to come out sooner or later. I did go down to the garage and take the coil wire out of both cars so she couldn't slip off while I was asleep and then I went to the living room and watched TV before going to bed.

The next morning, I got up and came downstairs to put the coffee on and I heard Hetty out in the garage running her battery down trying to start her car. I poured my coffee, sat down, and waited to see what she would do next. She only had two choices – come back in the house or start walking and unless she knocked on a neighbor's door and asked to use a phone, it was two miles to the nearest pay phone. Several minutes passed and then she came in the door from the garage and saw me sitting at the kitchen table and stopped. She was silent for several moments before saying, "My car won't start."

"Not surprising since I removed the coil wire."

"Why did you do that?"

"So you couldn't leave. You might want to avoid facing me for as long as you can, but I want to get it over with. You might as well sit down and tell me what you have been doing."

She stood there looking at me silently for almost a minute and then she walked over and sat down at the table.

Hetty had gone to the party and when it was clear that she had come alone and that I wouldn't be coming, Darrel, the guy she had kneed in the balls had slipped some date rape drug into her drink. Then he had taken her up to a hotel room, stripped her and fucked her. Then he had gone back to the party and had spread the word to all the other men who were there.

When the drug started to wear off and Hetty began to become aware, she found herself in the middle of a gangbang. By the time she had become clear headed, she had been fucked by twenty-one men, and by some more than once. Then Darrel had shown her the videotape he had made of the evening. Hetty's mind may not have known what was happening, but her body had and it had responded. As the drug wore off, she became a more active participant and by the time she was fully aware, her pussy was one raw nerve ending that craved what it was getting.

When she had called me to tell me not to worry, she was on her hands and knees and had a cock in her. The video that Darrel had taken showed her begging to be fucked, pleading for more cock, and even crawling across the floor on her hands and knees to get one. Then Darrel told her the price for my never seeing a copy of the video – she was to become his whore.

"You became his whore?"

"I couldn't let you see that tape, Brian. I looked like a cock crazy slut just begging guys to fuck me. You would never have believed that I wasn't doing it willingly. Toward the end I was, but you couldn't tell from the tape that I had been drugged at the start. He didn't tape the part where I just lay there and they used me, just the part where I got responsive."

"So, since the party, you have been fucking Darrel."

Hetty looked down at the table and in a weak, quiet voice said, "Him and whomever else he told me to."

I sat there and stared at her as she continued to look away from me. "He gives me to his friends and sometimes I have to entertain some of his better customers and at least once a week, I have to fuck the guys in the office on his desk. He tapes that too."

I made Hetty give me the names of everyone she could remember from the party and the names of everyone else she had been with since and then I put the coil wire back in her car, got it started and told her to go.

"What are you going to do?"

"I don't know yet."

"What should I do?"

"Hetty, you made your own choices when this started so you get to make your own choices now."

I left the garage and went back into the house.

I sat in my office staring at the wall trying to figure out what to do. Everything I could think of involved letting others know about what Hetty had done, but the more I thought about it, the more I thought "So what?" I already knew, so the only person who would really suffer when it came out would be Hetty and I wasn't feeling all that kindly toward her at the moment. With that thought in mind I made my decision.

I called a friend of mine who was a detective on the local police force and explained the situation to him and asked him for some advice. He told me he would give it some thought and get back to me. That night, things were a little strained around the house. I avoided talking to Hetty and when she tried to initiate sex in the evening, I rolled away from her. The next morning Hetty said, "I'm supposed to work late tonight; what should I do?"

"I told you yesterday, Hetty, you are making your own choices. If you aren't here tonight, I'll know what choice you made."

I wish things would have played out differently because I really would have liked to know what her choice would have been, but at ten that morning, my detective friend and his partner showed up at Hetty's place of employment. They asked for her boss and then had him point out Darrell and then in front of, and in the hearing of everyone in the office, they told Darrel they had a warrant for his arrest on charges of rape, pandering and a half a dozen other charges. They read him his rights, handcuffed him and then John had his partner take Darrel out and put him in the back of the cop car. Then John gave Hetty's boss a list of names and told him to get them all in a place where he could talk to them.

"You all know what is going on here and every one of you could face the same thing that Darrel is facing. You knew what he did that night and what he has done since and every one of you has contributed which makes all of you open to felony charges. But I don't want you. I want Darrel because I don't like assholes who drug women and then take advantage of them. I want Darrel so bad that I'm willing to forget about you people in exchange for your signed statements outlining what Darrel did and how he brought each of you in on it."

It was a bluff of course and if anyone there would have said that they wanted their lawyer, it would have been all over, but everyone was so eager to distance themselves from the mess that they fell over each other in the rush to get pens and paper. Then John took all the statements and went out to the squad car and had a talk with Darrel. He told Darrel that Hetty was pressing charges and then he showed Darrell all the signed statements.

"You are toast Darrel and if the charges that I read you weren't bad enough, you should think about this. Several of the customers that you made Hetty take care of were from out of state and that is enough to bring the Feds in on this. But there is a way out of this if you are smart enough to take it."

Hetty was waiting for me when I got home that night.

"How could you do that to me? How could you embarrass me in front of all the people that I work with? How can I go back in there and face them now?"

"Shouldn't be a problem. They were all happy enough to fuck you before so why shouldn't they be happy enough to fuck you in the future? Just keep giving them pussy sweetie and they will always be your friends. Here, this is for you," and I handed her a cardboard box.

"What's this?"

"It's all the tapes that Darrel made and eight thousand in cash that represents the commissions that Darrel made when he pimped you to his customers. It is my going away gift to you."

"Going away gift? What do you mean?"

"It means that our relationship is over."

"You can't! Brian I love you. I only did what I did to keep from losing you."

"No Hetty, if you loved me you would have trusted me enough to have told me what happened. You would have trusted me to know that it wasn't your fault. No, that's not quite right. It was your fault. I have warned you for years that your teasing was going to backfire on you some day. But that's neither here nor there. If you really loved me, you would have trusted me. My reading of the situation, given your sexual nature, is that it happened and even though it was forced on you to start with, you enjoyed it and you saw Darrel's blackmail as a way for you to try other men and have an excuse if you got caught. I might be wrong, but then it doesn't matter. The bottom line for me is that you didn't love me enough to trust me and I can't live with that."

I stood up and pushed the box across the table to her, "My lawyer will be in touch," and I left her sitting at the kitchen table as I left the house.

Julie Hanson

Charlie Hanson sat in his work cubicle and stared at his computer screen. His mind really wasn't at work. No, in fact his mind was 27.3 miles away at the little two-bedroom ranch at 1346 Morningside Drive. Specifically, his thoughts were in the master bedroom where eighty-seven minutes previous he had left his wife Julie crying on their bed. The argument they'd had was just one more born out of the frustrations of the past two months.

Charlie could barely remember the last time they had made love. For almost two months he had heard the litany – "I've got a headache." "My stomach is upset." "I just don't feel well." "It's my time of the month."

This morning had finally torn it for him. Just before he left the house he told her not to wait dinner on him and when she had asked why, he said, "Since I can't get laid at home I'm going to try and find myself a woman to pick up. If I can't score that way maybe I'll hire a prostitute," and he had stormed out of the house.

Charlie knew the root of the problem. When Julie had found out she was pregnant, she had been overjoyed. When three months later she had miscarried, she had been devastated. The doctor told him that some depression was normal after such a circumstance, but that Julie would snap out of it in a week or two. Well, she hadn't, and when Charlie told her she should seek some professional help she had refused saying that there was nothing wrong with her. That morning, when she had roughly pushed his hands away from her breast he had finally had enough and he had lost his cool because of it.

~~***~~

How Charlie managed to get any work done that day was a mystery, but somehow he had managed to clear out his 'in' basket and at 5 p.m. he found himself wondering what to do. He'd said that he wouldn't be home after work and while he regretted saying it, and wished to hell he hadn't, he was not going to go home until late. He had no intention of finding another woman. He loved Julie too much to do that to her, but he had to make her think he was serious. Maybe, just maybe, it would shake her out of her funk.

"God knows we can't go on this way," he thought.

At the elevator he ran into Tom Combs from accounting. "Charlie! How's the boy?"

"Fine Tom, yourself?"

"Couldn't be better Charlie, couldn't be better. Just been promoted to section manager. I'm going to stop at the Back Door for a few celebratory toddies. Care to join me?"

Charlie's problem of what to do now solved, he sat with Tom at the Back Door Lounge and considered the irony of the situation. He'd told Julie he was going to find a woman and even though he did not intend to the place was just crawling with women on the prowl. He caught several inviting glances and did his best to ignore them.

"It's too bad that we are both happily married Charlie," said Tom, "We could get laid in a hurry."

One absolutely gorgeous redhead with sparkling green eyes had even come to the table, looked him right in the eye and said, "Buy me a drink, dance with me, take me home, your choice."

Charlie had choked on his drink, laughed and said, "Why did this never happen to me before I got married?"

Tom and the redhead had both laughed and as she turned to go back to her table she said, "Think about it, I'll be her for a while."

Charlie did think about it. He thought about it long and hard, but in the end his love for Julie won out.

When Charlie got home, Julie was in bed, either asleep or pretending to be, and she did not move when he slipped into bed beside her. In the morning, Julie ignored him and he made no effort to talk to her. It was another long day for him at work as his mind was not on his work, but on Julie and what was going on with them. He got his paycheck at lunchtime and ran down to the corner bank to cash it. He put the usual ten percent in savings, took $150 cash back and put the rest in his checking account. On the way home that night, he considered ways to mend fences with Julie and thought that maybe he should look into getting some professional help. A marriage counselor perhaps or maybe even a psychiatrist. When he walked in the back door however, Julie greeted him with a sneer.

"Welcome home stud. How's the tomcat tonight? Didn't stop on the way home for a quickie from some slut?"

"Fuck you!" Charlie said as he walked through the kitchen on the way to his den. He heard Julie run upstairs crying and he was tempted to run after her, but then decided that it would be a sign of weakness at a time when he felt he needed to remain strong.

In the kitchen, on the counter next to the electric can opener, was a little glass jar where every payday Charlie would put $75 for Julie to use as her mad money. Because of the way things had gone on his arrival the night before, he had not put the money in the jar. When he awoke Saturday morning and went downstairs, Julie was already in the kitchen.

"Where's my money? My hair appointment is for 9:30 and I need to get going."

The tone of her voice pissed Charlie off and he said, "You don't get any this week. If I have to pay for the sex that I supposed to be able to get from you, you are going to be the one who pays for it."

~~***~~

The next week was a very frosty one for Charlie. There did not seem to be any way he could get himself out of the hole that he and Julie were both digging. Everything he said, everything she said, just made everything worse. When Friday came and he got home from work and was getting ready to put the money in the jar for Julie he noticed the note on the counter:

"Gone out to make some money. Don't bother waiting up."

Charlie did not intend to wait up – he wouldn't give her the satisfaction – but he found that he couldn't sleep. He tossed and turned and was still awake when he heard a car pull into the drive. When Julie did not come in for several minutes, he got out of bed and went to the window to look out. He did not recognize the car, but there was no mistaking that it was Julie sitting on the front seat kissing some man that Charlie had never seen before. He saw them break the embrace and then Julie got out of the car and headed for the house. Charlie got back in bed and pretended to be asleep when Julie came into the room. When she got in bed she smelled strongly of alcohol and cigarettes. Charlie did not sleep well that night.

In the morning, Charlie's attempts at conversation met with silence, but he kept after Julie until finally she said, "You want to know where I was? Okay, I'll tell you. You spent my money on whores so I decided to get it back and you know how I did it? I went down to the Shamrock bar and picked up a guy, took him to a hotel and fucked him. And you want to know something else? You must have spent my money in the low rent district because I got $200 for my pussy. How do you like those apples asshole!?"

"Bullshit!" said Charlie.

"Oh yeah? Well just take a look at this."

Julie opened up her handbag and took out a fist full of money and threw it down on the table in front of Charlie and he saw at least $600.

"That's right shit head. Three guys apiece for $200 and a blowjob for $75."

"No way, you couldn't do something like that."

"Oh yes, I can and I'm going to do it again tonight."

"I don't believe a word of this. I don't know where you got the money, but you aren't going to get me to believe that you are selling yourself."

"I'll tell you what sport. I'll save money on a hotel room tonight. I'll bring my customers home with me and you can watch me fuck them on your bed," and the she left the room.

~~***~~

That afternoon, Charlie watched as Julie put on her nylons and stepped into her heels. She did not put on a bra and the dress she wore left little to the imagination. When she left, she looked him right in the eye and told him that she wouldn't be long. The cab was already waiting and she got in it and was gone. Twenty minutes later, the phone rang and when Charlie answered it was Julie.

"I told my date that my husband likes to watch and he said he didn't like that kinky kind of stuff so if you want to watch, you'll have to hide in the closet."

Charlie started to tell her that things had gone far enough and to just come on home, but she had already hung up on him.

Ten minutes passed and Charlie spent the entire time looking out the front window. A strange car pulled into the drive and pulled up to the house. Julie and a man he had never seen before got out of the car and headed for the front door. Charlie did not believe what he was seeing, but it was there. Surely it was just a joke. She had found somebody to help her pull a joke on him.

"Okay," he thought, "I'll play along," and he dashed upstairs and made a place for himself in the closet leaving just enough of the door open to give him a view of the bed. He smiled to himself, "I wonder how she will handle it when I don't come rushing out of the closet and play the jealous husband?"

Minutes later, Julie entered the room with her 'customer' and walked directly over to the bed. She smiled at the man and said, "You can put the money over there on the dresser."

The man took out a wad of bills, put several on the dresser and returned the rest to his pocket.

"Nice touch," thought Charlie, "I'll bet they rehearsed that on the way to the house."

Julie slowly stripped off her dress and did a slow turn in front of the man. "What do you think?"

"Nice, very nice," the man said as he started to remove his clothes.

Charlie thought that standing there with her bare tits showing was going a little far for a joke. He knew that she was waiting for him to rush out of the closet and break things up, but he was not going to give her the satisfaction. She was going to have to be the one to call things off. He was going to sit tight and see just how far she would go before ending the farce.

The man was down to his boxers and Charlie could see that the man had a hard on. Well, there would be no way of avoiding that. You could rehearse all you wanted, but there was no way a normal man could look at Julie the way she was standing there and not become erect. The man dropped his boxers and his erect cock quivered and pointed at Julie like a bird dog pointing to a covey of quail. He walked to the bed and sat down. Julie turned to face him and, with a long look at the closet, she stepped out of her panties.

"That's my signal," thought Charlie, "but I'm not breaking. She has to end it herself."

Julie knelt down in front of the man and still looking at the closet she opened her mouth and swallowed the man's cock. Ice gripped Charlie's heart. When Julie's mouth closed on the man's cock, Charlie finally realized that everything that Julie had told him was true. He watched his marriage die as Julie's mouth moved up and down on the man's cock. She sucked on it for several minutes and then he watched numbly as Julie got on the bed and spread her legs for her 'john'.

For the next twenty minutes, Charlie watched as the two on the bed shifted into various positions as the man fucked Julie. Charlie became aware of his own body's sensations. He looked down and saw that he had opened his fly and was stroking his own erect cock. He heard loud noises and his attention shifted back to the bed. Julie was having an orgasm and her customer was gasping, "I'm cumming, I'm cumming," and then he gave a little groan and it was over.

The customer got off the bed and started putting on his clothes. He looked over at Julie who was lying on the bed with her legs still spread wide, pussy hair wet with cum, runs in her nylons and a satisfied smile on her face.

"I've got your number. I will definitely call you the next time I'm in town. You are well worth the price."

Dressed, he pulled out his wad of bills and placed one on the dresser. "A little something extra. I'll let myself out."

When she heard the front door close and the man's car start Julie called out, "You can come out now."

As Charlie emerged from the closet, Julie noticed his hard on and smiled. "Bring that over here and let Julie take care of it for you. No charge of course."

Charlie climbed on the bed and Julie took his cock in her right hand and guided him into her. "Did you like it? Did you like seeing your wife fuck for money? Your cock liked it, I can tell. Tell me you liked it baby, tell me you liked it."

Charlie was silent, but his cock spoke for him. It had never felt so hard and, he admitted to himself as he slid in and out of Julie's cum filled pussy, it had never felt so good. He hadn't had sex in almost three months, but he had jacked off a lot while waiting for Julie to finally agree to have sex with him so he didn't cum quick. In fact, he couldn't seem to cum at all. He fucked Julie for what felt like half an hour, but he couldn't seem to cum. Julie had at least four orgasms and he was beginning to think he was never going to get off when at last he felt the pressure flood to the head of his cock and he screamed as he pumped his cum into her already full cunt. He held himself over her until his cock deflated and then he fell onto the bed next to her. He spent a minute catching his breath and when he looked over at Julie, she was staring at him with amazement on her face.

"Jesus Charlie, what came over you? Did you really get that turned on watching me fuck that guy?"

"How could you? You denied me sex for months and then at the drop of a hat you go out and fuck men for money. Why did you refuse me when it was so obviously easy for you to do it?"

Julie just shrugged her shoulders.

"Why? Why did you do that to me Julie?"

"Why? You want to know why? Because you went out and spent my mad money on a whore. You can't know how much that hurt me. I had to find a way to get back at you. Some way that would hurt you as much as you hurt me."

Charlie looked at her and slowly shook his head as he started to get out of bed. "I didn't spend your money on a whore. You should have known that I loved you too much to ever do something like that to you."

"Don't lie to me," snapped Julie.

"I'm not lying to you Julie. I spent the evening having drinks with Tom Combs to celebrate his promotion and then I came home. I've never even looked at another woman since I married you."

He heard Julie wail, "Oh my God. Oh God, what have I done!"

Just before Charlie left the room he turned and looked at Julie.

"I'll tell you what you have done Julie. You ended your marriage and found a way to support yourself at the same time."

And then Charlie headed for the basement to get the suitcases he would start to pack.

The End

Here is a preview of the next book in the series:

JUST PLAIN BOB

Hazardous Wives

HOT EROTICA
BECOMING A SHARED WIFE, VOL. 2

What happened was my own fault, so I guess I can't cry too loud. But Adrianne gets a little bit of the blame – she didn't have to do what she did. It all happened because I'm a basically insecure guy where my wife is concerned. Adrianne is drop dead gorgeous and had every guy in town hot after her ass from the age of fourteen on. I, on the other hand, was the type of nerd who never even could get a date until I hit the eleventh grade. How I ended up with Adrianne, I'll never know; but I was constantly afraid that other guys would try and take her away from me and that someday she might just realize she had made a mistake and let one of them do it. Add to that, a generally suspicious nature and an active imagination and you had the recipe for disaster.

~~***~~

Adrianne and I had been married just a little over three years and up until a month ago I didn't have any reason to believe that she was untrue to me. But all of a sudden, things just started to seem different, you know? I couldn't tell exactly what it was, but it seemed as if Adrianne's body was sending out signals that said, "I'm fucking around." Nothing obvious, nothing that I could see, hear, taste, or touch, just a feeling. So I set out to find out one way or another.

She went out one night a week with her girlfriends and I was out two nights a week bowling. We had a lot of friends who came over to our house a lot, especially on the nights I was out, so those were the times I would have to concentrate on to find out what she was doing. For four weeks I followed her every night she went out with the girls, but all they ever did was meet at someone's place and drink beer and shoot the shit. Once, they went to an Avon party. But none of those nights did I ever see any guys around.

At the same time I was checking on Adrianne's nights out, I was also keeping a close eye on the people that hung out around our house. Most of them were Adrianne's friend and some of them I didn't very much like. I figured if she was doing anything it was probably with one of them. I told the guys on the teams I bowled on that I had some personal problems that needed looking after and told them I would have to sit out for maybe a month. Next, I hit the liquor store and stocked up on what we usually had in the house and stashed it under a tarp in the garage and waited.

The first opportunity came the very first week that I followed her on her girls' night out. It was the next night, which was usually my bowling night, and I had driven a couple of blocks away and then come back to the house. I had already fixed the blinds on every window in the house so I could see in from outside and I got into position and watched. The usual crowd of about eight or ten were there and nothing at all had happened by ten o'clock at which time people started leaving.

Pretty soon the crowd had dwindled to four people and Adrianne - Doug, his wife Mary, Gregg and Tom. I saw Mary slip into the bedroom with Gregg and I saw Doug watch them go. I'd heard that Doug and Mary had an "open marriage" but I had never known for sure. I moved to the bedroom window and looked in to see Mary sucking Gregg's cock, but it wasn't Mary that I was interested in.

To purchase the book, look for **Hazardous Wives - Becoming a Shared Wife, Vol. 2.**

Here is a preview of **Becoming a Shared Wife, Vol. 1.**

JUST PLAIN BOB

Wife

Sharing

and Other Adventures

HOT EROTICA

BECOMING A SHARED WIFE, VOL. 1

Abby

You never know who your friends really are until you give them a chance to take advantage of you.

Abby and I had been married a little over ten years and it had been a great ten. The two of us always seemed to be on the same page no matter what we did. It was almost as if we could read each other's minds over a distance. An example: One morning I was getting ready to go to work and I noticed that I need new underwear. I made a mental note to pick up some the next time I went to the store.

When I got home that night I found out that Abby had gone shopping and had purchased me some new briefs. She had stopped at Target to get some sheets that were on sale and for some reason that she hadn't understood she had grabbed me some underwear. Another time I was on the way home from work and instead of turning right onto our street I kept going straight. I don't know why I did it because I had no real reason not to make my turn. Whatever the reason, I was almost at Safeway when I decided to turn back, but at the last minute I turned into the Safeway parking lot and went into the store. I had a sudden desire for spaghetti and meat sauce and I went inside and got the stuff I needed to make it.

When I got home, Abby called me on the phone just as I came in the door, "Do you mind if we go out for dinner tonight? I've had a craving for spaghetti all day and I don't have what we need to make at the house." Those are only two of the examples of how in tune with each other we are and there are many, many more.

Abby and I met in college, started dating, fell in love and we got married. We were both virgins when we tied the knot, Abby because she had promised her mother on her deathbed, and me because I had been too painfully shy to get anywhere with a girl. But even though we started out inexperienced, our sex life was a full and rich one. Again, our being in tune with each other had a lot to do with it. I instinctively knew when and where she wanted to be touched and how and she knew the same about me.

As a gag gift, one of her sisters had given her a box labeled "Sexual Instruction Manual" at her bridal shower and when Abby opened it she found a porno tape. For the first month of our marriage we played that tape over and over and did everything that we saw on that tape. We did oral, anal, and sixty-nine; we did missionary position, doggie style, several of the more acrobatic positions and in general had a grand old time.

We decided to buy more porno tapes and became frequent customers of the adult bookstore down town. We also had a large collection of dildos that we used in role playing, a sex swing hanging from the beams in the basement and a dozen different bottles of lotions and ointments. When it came to role-playing, Abby's favorite was to believe she was getting fucked by two men at the same time. While I stroked into her ass, she would use a dildo on her pussy and she always seemed to have a larger than average orgasm when we did that.

Once, during a light hearted moment, I asked her if she was ever going to drag another man home with her so she could do it for real. She blushed and said, "Good God no. I'm a married woman, not a slut. I could never do it with anyone I didn't know and if I did it with someone I know I would never be able to face them again." Being as tuned in to her as I was I knew that she meant it.

After ten years of marriage our sex life was still going gangbusters. We enjoyed sex six and seven times a week and it surprised us to hear that most of our married friends, who had been married as long as we had, were only having sex twice a week if even that. We had stopped buying porno tapes, but were still getting ideas from magazines like Penthouse Letters, Penthouse Forum and Gallery.

On a trip to Mexico we made love on the little balcony outside our room. Abby leaned over the railing while I fucked her from behind. Several people saw us and knew what we were doing and they waved at us and Abby waved back. Another time we made love in the ladies room of a local bar while there was a line of women waiting outside and she sucked my dick in a stall in a men's room while other guys came in and took their whiz just feet away from us. Life was not dull for us - not ever!

It was my thirty-fifth birthday and Abby threw me a surprise party at one of the local bars. When I got home from work that night, Abby said she wanted to eat out. I asked her where and she said the Watering Hole.

"I have a craving for one of their half pound ground rounds with a big slice of Bermuda onion."

We walked into the bar and the surprise was complete and we settled down to party. It was a Friday night and the Hole had a band so the drinking and dancing were unrestrained. As the birthday boy, everyone wanted to buy me a drink and around eleven I started feeling a little woozy and by midnight I was passed out. Abby had been putting it away too, but she wasn't quite as bad off as I was. There were a couple of people who thought they were fairly sober and they loaded me into a car to take me home.

I vaguely remember coming out of my alcohol induced stupor at one point to see Abby in only high heels and nylons being passed around by a group of guys who were kissing her and copping feels. It looked like she was protesting but I faded out without knowing.

I woke up the next morning with a head that felt like a bass drum being pounded on. My mouth tasted like a cavalry regiment had ridden through it and as I stumbled to the bathroom I swore that I would never drink again.

Finishing in the bathroom, I went into the bedroom and found Abby asleep on the bed. There was dried cum everywhere. She had love bites on her tits, her legs were spread and I could see cum leaking out of her pussy lips, which were red and swollen. She had one high heel on and only god knew where the other one was; her nylons had runs and cum stains all over them and it was obvious that she had been well used. I looked down at her and wondered what the previous night had done to our life.

I managed to get to the kitchen and get the coffee going without having to rush to the bathroom and little by little I began to return to the land of the living.

About two hours later, I heard the shower start running and I knew that Abby was awake. I was sitting on the bed when she came out of the shower and when she saw me she started crying…

Purchase the book in Amazon, Wife Sharing and Other Adventures - Becoming a Shared Wife, Vol. 1.

Also by this Author:

The Prodigal Family: The Abbotts

Watching My Shared Wife

The Waitress and the Runaway Husband

Baiting Mr. Little

Too Hot for Henry

Chuck's Fantasy

Wife Sharing and Other Adventures

From the Author

If you enjoyed any of my books then please share the love and promote my books in Amazon.

If you write me a review and send me an email I will send you a free book, or many.
(Just know that these emails are filtered by my publisher.)

Good news is always welcome.

One Last Thing, For Kindle Readers...

When you turn the page, Kindle will give you the opportunity to rate this book and share your thoughts on Facebook and Twitter. If you enjoyed my writings, would you please take a few seconds to let your friends know about it? Because... when they enjoy they will be grateful to you and so will I.

Thank You!

An Open Letter from Just Plain Bob

A message for those who like my stories, those who hate my stories, those who are indifferent and those who have yet to make up their minds.

I have often stated that I really don't care what others think about my stories, that I write for my own enjoyment and then I offer to share. If you like my stories fine and if you don't, also fine since I have already satisfied my target audience - me!

It is human nature to strive to get better. If you take up bowling your first games are going low scoring, but you will work and practice to get better and as your average climbs you may forget the game where you had three gutter balls and shot an eighty-six, but that game is still there in your past.

Your first time on the golf course you shot an eighty on the front nine, but did you settle for that being your game or did you work to improve? You may eventually get a three handicap, but that nine hole eighty is still there as part of your past.

When you hired in at your job did you say, "Cool, I got it made" and do nothing more than what you barely had to do or did you go to work thinking that, "Someday I'm going to be running this place." You might never climb that high, but human nature says that you are going to at least try.

It is the same with authors who write stories and post them on sites like Literotica. Their first stories might not be all that good, but comments and feedback along with a desire to get better drive them toward putting out a better product or to at least try.

I'm no different. My first stories might not have been all that great, but they are still there on the hard drive. I like cheating wife stories and five years ago I found my first adult site that catered to cheating wife stories. It was a pay site, but it had a policy of giving a free lifetime membership to anyone who submitted five stories to the site. How hard can that be I said to myself as I sat down and fired up the word processor and went to work.

I sent my five stories in and sat back to enjoy my free membership and a funny thing happened. I started getting feedback, most of it positive, and I became hooked. I started cranking out more stories. The site I was sending my stories to had seven categories:

Bisexual
Cream Pie
Groups

I Watch
Gang Bang
Racial
SM/BD

I know nothing about bisexual or SM/BD and I had no interest in Groups so all the stories I wrote I tailored for the four remaining categories:

Cream Pie
I Watch
Gang Bang
Racial.

I turned out eight stories a month, two for each category, which means that after five years I have over 120 stories in each of those categories and they are all still on the hard drive.

A year ago I received an email asking me why I never posted stories on Literotica. The answer? I didn't know about Lit. I pulled it up, liked what I saw, and started sending in stories to it. All new stories? No, not hardly, not with over 400 stories sitting on the hard drive. Maybe one new story for each fifteen or so old ones. The newer ones are better, at least I think they are and I have received some feedback that leads me to believe that others think so too, and I will continue to write new ones.

But I am still going to recycle what is on the hard drive, stories that were written specifically to fit the four categories. That means that those of you who hate cream pie stories still have eighty or so to look forward to. Ditto for those who call me a racist; you will get another seventy or so interracial stories.

Those who hate wimps will only see about fifty more of those because the stories I sent to the I Watch category were split 50/50 between what some call wimps and some call "real men." Why the 50/50 split? It came from listening to the readers. I would get feedback asking me why all the men in my stories were hard asses. "In real life men are more forgiving, especially if it is the first indiscretion." So I would write stories with forgiving husbands and boyfriends and then the next batch of feedback would say, "Why are all your husbands spineless wimps" and I'd write stories that went back the other way.

Eventually I came to realize that I was wasting my time - there was no way I could write a story that would satisfy everybody and that is when I adopted my philosophy of writing for my own enjoyment and then offering to share.

As far as the gangbang stories? Well, what can I say? Gangbangs are gangbangs and there are still eighty or so of them to go.

The bottom line is that Literotica readers are going to see more of my old stories than my new ones. If I'm still around three or four years from now it will probably go the other way, more new than old.

I feel the need to respond to some of the comments and emails I have received. By far the largest percentage comes from people who say, "You are an asshole because all women are not whores and sluts and that's all you make them out to be."

Next most common is, "You must really hate women you sick fuck."

"You must be a wimp because all the men in your stories are wimps" is up there in the top ten along with, "Why don't you give it a rest and go crawl off in a hole somewhere."

There is a lot more, but I'm only going to address those four and in reverse order.

I won't stop and go crawl in a hole because I am enjoying the hell out of what I am doing and remember what I said, I am doing this for MY OWN ENJOYMENT and then I offer to share. Some obviously like my sharing with them and so I will continue to do so. No one is holding a gun to a reader's head and telling them they must click on a Just Plain Bob story or die. It is a conscious choice on the reader's part to move that mouse and click on that story.

When a man finds out he has a cheating wife or girlfriend there are only a limited number of ways he can handle it. If he loves her he can forgive, try to forget and try to hold on and somehow make things work. He can turn his back on her, walk away and get on with his life. The third option is to take revenge.

According to a good portion of those who send me feedback the first and second options are proof that the men are wimps. If the man takes the third option he is still considered a wimp if he doesn't do some sort of physical damage to the woman and her lover. These readers believe that the only way not to be a wimp is to kill, maim and destroy everything in sight. Doing that however, will invariably get the man throw in jail and that is why it so rarely happens in real life.

In real life most revenge takes place in the man's head when he says to himself, "I should have _____ (fill in the blank) the fucking cunt!" I know this because I have been there and done that (see The Dark Trilogy). In my stories I try to mirror real life so kill, maim and destroy are going to be for the most part absent. Outside of some fisticuffs there will be very little physical violence in my stories. Most of my husbands are going to do what I did, what several of my friends and others that I know have done, forgive, or walk away. If this makes them wimps and me a wimp for writing the story that way, so be it.

Next is the "I must hate all women." Nothing could be farther from the truth. I love women. I lust after women. I even like whores and sluts. I have been married four times, engaged two other times (that did not end in marriage) and I have always had girlfriends between marriages. My philosophy is that women were put on this earth for me to enjoy and I'm not talking just sexually. I could sit at the mall (and have) for hours and just girl watch.

The engagements, girlfriends and three of the four marriages bring me to the #1 anti JPB comment on the list.

"You are an asshole because all women aren't whores and sluts."

Well dear reader, you can not prove that by me! I will say up front that I KNOW all women aren't whores and sluts, BUT the majority of the women in my life were. My mother ran around on my father for years while he was driving a truck for a living. My Aunt Margaret cheated regularly on my Uncle Bill, as did my Aunt Mildred on my Uncle Paul. My Aunt Betty fucked around on my Uncle Bob for years and finally left him for his brother, my Uncle Wendell. Uncle Wendell in turn caught her on her knees at his company Christmas party giving Season's Greetings to his boss.

My sister is three times divorced and each divorce came about when the then current husband caught her out spreading pollen. Both of the engagements I mentioned ended when I found out that I was not the one and only and a lot of the girls I dated between marriages never made it to engagement status for the same reason.

And that brings me to my three ex-wives. The first one, Helen (I believe I commented on her in the intro to The Dark Trilogy) had seven different lovers before I found out what was going on. I was living proof that love is blind. Ditto with my second wife. She had a secret life that she hid from me and when I found out about her brother, his friends and the gangbangs she was history.

My third marriage ended in divorce because of a different kind of cheating (and I can just imagine the outrage I am going to get over this) - she cheated on me with an idea. I was away from home on business, she was lonely, a couple of Jehovah's Witnesses knocked on the door and my wife, with nothing better to do invited them in. When I came home from my trip I found out that she had found God. On a scale that runs from TRUE BELIEVER on one end to ATHEIST on the other you will find me just to the right of AGNOSTIC and since I would not allow myself to be SAVED the marriage eventually died.

So yes, I write about sluts and whores because as everyone knows, you tend to write about the things you know. And I do like sluts and whores, just not the ones that lie to me and cheat on me.

So be forewarned - if you click on a Just Plain Bob story you will be getting sluts, whores and husbands who do not kill, maim and destroy. There are other things you will rarely find in a Just Plain Bob story. Even though I try to mirror real life my stories all take place in StoryLand. In StoryLand STDs and unwanted pregnancies do not exist unless the author feels like they may add something to the story. Bad things do not happen in StoryLand unless the author so wills it and no amount of "You should have..." in comments and feedback will change a story already posted.

Lastly, I will touch on a truth. None of what I have written here means shit because the same readers will still read the same stories that they profess to hate and make the same comments they have always made. Knowing this, I will deliberately post stories that will have them frothing at the mouth.

It is the least I can do for an adoring public.

Thank you!

Just Plain Bob
justplainbob@awesomeauthors.org